CHASING THE EARL

The Arrogant Earls
Book Two

Kathleen Ayers

ARE YOU SIGNED UP FOR DRAGONBLADE'S BLOG?

You'll get the latest news and information on exclusive giveaways, exclusive excerpts, coming releases, sales, free books, cover reveals and more.

Check out our complete list of authors, too!

No spam, no junk. That's a promise!

Sign Up Here

www.dragonbladepublishing.com

Dearest Reader;

Thank you for your support of a small press. At Dragonblade Publishing, we strive to bring you the highest quality Historical Romance from some of the best authors in the business. Without your support, there is no 'us', so we sincerely hope you adore these stories and find some new favorite authors along the way.

Happy Reading!

CEO, Dragonblade Publishing

Additional Dragonblade books by Author Kathleen Ayers

The Arrogant Earls Series
Forgetting the Earl (Book 1)
Chasing the Earl (Book 2)

CHAPTER ONE

A S A RULE, Miss Emmagene Stitch didn't care for weddings or house parties.

Unfortunately, she was on her way to both.

Not two separate events, thankfully, but one overblown, pretentious affair that would combine two of her least favorite things. Weddings reminded Emmagene of love, which in turn soured her stomach, since she'd dispensed with the belief in such an emotion years ago. House parties were just a particular form of torture, especially for an older, unmarried woman, which Emmagene was. Forced intimacy with a group of people with whom she had nothing in common and who wouldn't be pleased to find Emmagene in their midst. Spinsters, which she often declared herself to be, were viewed as an oddity with no specific function. If the entire event weren't culminating in the marriage of her dearest friend and cousin, Honora Drevenport Culpepper, to the Earl of Southwell, she would stay home with a pot of tea and a good book.

"Have a lovely time, dear." Mama pecked Emmagene on the cheek before sending her out the door, envy stamped clearly on her pretty features. "Are you certain—"

"I am, Mama." Emmagene adjusted the ribbons of her bonnet. "You weren't invited. It isn't as if I can sneak you into my trunk as an unpleasant surprise for Honora. Do I need to keep reminding you?"

"Yes, but dear, if you would only speak to your cousin." Her mother's beringed fingers twisted about as Emmagene strode to the door. "I could be packed and join you in a day or two? Surely Honora will capitulate if you just ask her? I was only doing as Agnes wished and meant no disrespect toward my niece."

Emmagene pulled on her gloves, rolling her eyes at the mention of her aunt and Honora's mother, Agnes Drevenport. "Just because Aunt Agnes decided not to receive her own daughter didn't mean you had to follow suit. The scandal wasn't Honora's fault."

"Yes, but the circumstances are now greatly changed. I regret my earlier actions. As does your Aunt Agnes."

"Because Honora is to be a countess. How that must chafe Aunt Agnes to have her own daughter, the future Lady Southwell, turn her away. Think of the gossip." Emmagene's eyes widened. She hadn't an ounce of pity for her aunt. "She's treated Honora terribly her entire life. The talk over Southwell only gave her another reason to do so."

"You played a part in the gossip as well, Emmagene. Yet you are still being asked to attend."

Emmagene paused at her mother's words, hating the truth of them. She had unwittingly helped Lord Tarrington and Loretta Culpepper, Honora's former mother-in-law, in the disparagement of her cousin's reputation, nearly destroying Honora's relationship with Southwell in the process.

"Honora has forgiven me." Southwell probably never would, though he was sending his coach to collect her for the journey to his estate, Longwood, where the house party would take place.

"Exactly, which is why if you only asked—"

"I will not, Mother. Not for you and not for Aunt Agnes."

Her mother pursed her lips, which signaled a lecture, one Emmagene was in no mood for. "You are so very *hard*, Emmagene."

She supposed she was, at least in her mother's estimation. "I'm sorry you feel that way, Mother. You and Aunt Agnes can spend the week I'm gone sipping tea and weeping over the fact all of London knows the new Lady Southwell refuses to receive either of you. You've no one to blame but yourselves. Neither of you had the decency to even apologize for the way you treated her. You had no interest in Honora until her impending marriage to an earl was announced."

"That is unfair," came her mother's weak reply.

Emmagene didn't think so. She marched off in the direction of the coach waiting for her, a magnificent conveyance bearing the Southwell coat of arms and pulled by a team of matching snow-white horses. While she didn't trust Southwell, or any gentleman as a rule, Emmagene had to admit Southwell possessed excellent taste in coaches.

Emmagene stretched her fingers over the red leather squabs as she settled herself inside the coach with the help of Southwell's footman. Pity she wasn't taking this coach somewhere more inviting than a house party hosted by Lady Trent.

Lady Trent didn't care for Emmagene. Not a whit.

Which was fine. Really, it was.

The coach jerked forward, and Emmagene glanced back at her parents' three-story home of rough gray stone. She could just make out the pale oval of her mother's face as she watched Emmagene pull away from the drawing room window. Mother was probably, even now, dashing off a note to her elder sister, Agnes, to inform her that despite pleading, Emmagene had gone off to the Earl of Southwell's estate and Honora's wedding alone.

Her mother thought it the gravest of sins to be a woman alone.

With a shake of her head, Emmagene smoothed down the skirts of her walnut-brown traveling dress and opened her book. Longwood was barely a full day's ride from London but somewhat isolated in the country. She planned to doze a bit or read. The novel she'd brought was a frothy bit of fluff complete with a handsome gentleman rescuing a young lady in distress, something Emmagene would normally never read under any circumstances, but Honora had sent it to her. At the very least, it was sure to provide Emmagene some amusement.

Love. A word gentlemen cooed into young ladies' ears so they would give up their virtue with little resistance.

She knew from experience.

The coach was in motion for several minutes before taking a sharp turn down a narrow treelined street. She peered out the window, trying to get her bearings. The street itself didn't look familiar, though the homes, all richly appointed, told Emmagene the neighborhood was an affluent one. No matter how lovely the area, the coach should be headed in the opposite direction. If Southwell meant to rid himself of Honora's sharp-tongued cousin, as Emmagene had heard him refer to her, he might do better to leave her in a less prestigious area of London.

She rapped on the roof to summon the driver. "I don't believe this is the way out of town."

"Lady Trent requested we pick up another guest for the wedding, miss," the driver informed her. "We'll only be a moment."

How curious. And she'd assumed Southwell had sent the coach, not Lady Trent. Possibly they were retrieving a relation who could not find their own transportation to Longwood for some reason. According to Honora, Southwell, though an only child, had a large extended family with dozens of first, second, and third cousins.

Wonderful.

A bit of warning would have been appropriate. Now Emmagene would be forced to make pleasant conversation with some elderly aunt or lecherous great-uncle of Southwell's. A simple-minded cousin, perhaps, or a spinster much like herself. Not that there was anything at all wrong with being unwed. When Emmagene had reached the exalted age of twenty-five, after three unsuccessful seasons, Aunt Agnes had promptly declared Emmagene a spinster with no hope of ever marrying. It was the only thing she and Aunt Agnes had ever agreed upon.

Emmagene peered out the window as the coach rolled to a

stop before a red brick three-story home. A bit of paint had peeled away from the front door, enough to curl and form a spiral. Twin urns, one cracked, sat on either side of the entrance, two small shrubs struggling for life from their depths. The overall impression was one of careless neglect.

Her traveling companion was bound to be old and musty if they resided here.

Emmagene shut her eyes. It might be best to pretend to be asleep. If she were lucky, she could get away with the act for several hours.

"My lord," she heard the driver address Southwell's relative, dashing Emmagene's hopes of an elderly aunt. Lecherous uncle it was.

"Just the one small trunk," the man, whose voice was a gritty baritone, curtly informed the driver and footman before the coach door was unceremoniously thrown open.

Emmagene opened her eyes, just a slit.

A very broad, very male torso filled the entire doorway of the coach. A purple wine stain screamed at her from his waistcoat. The scent of stale cigars filled her nostrils, along with the nauseating aroma of cheap perfume.

Good lord. He smells like a brothel. Or at least how Emmagene imagined a brothel would smell. She'd never actually visited one, of course.

A massive booted foot came into view as Southwell's relative pushed his oversize shoulders into the coach, clutching the sides of the vehicle with his hands. Which were ungloved and so large Emmagene didn't wonder that he couldn't find gloves to fit him.

A tangled mass of hair, the same color as tarnished brass, followed the shoulders as he took the seat across from her, rocking the coach with his substantial weight.

No. Anyone but him.

This was bound to be unpleasant; in fact, Emmagene considered dashing from the coach and just hiring a hack to take her to Southwell's estate rather than endure *this* gentleman's company.

Rude. Ill mannered. Completely self-absorbed. Indiscreet in his affairs, which were purported to be numerous. Apparently, his boorish behavior didn't put women off. But it could have just as easily been his wealth that attracted them.

She'd completely forgotten he and Southwell were related. Or perhaps Emmagene had only chosen to block it from her mind.

The Earl of Huntly ran his fingers through his hair, dislodging several curls, unconcerned that in addition to not wearing gloves, as a proper gentleman should, he also wasn't wearing a hat. The only thing remotely pleasing about Huntly was his eyes. Like the sapphires in her mother's favorite pair of earrings and framed by thick inky-black lashes.

"Switch seats with me," he said.

Emmagene had once had the misfortune of being introduced to Huntly. Briefly. He hadn't taken her hand at the time but had instead grunted in her general direction by way of greeting before dismissing her as being of little importance. "I beg your pardon?"

"I become a bit green if I take this seat. Even more so after the night I've had. You sit here. I'll sit there," he continued. "It's fairly simple. What don't you understand? Are you addled?" He had the audacity to snap his oversize fingers at her.

"Oh, I understand you completely, my lord," she assured him. "I just have no desire to change my seat. I'm comfortable where I am."

It was clear he didn't remember having been introduced, even more apparent he hadn't the inclination to be the least polite. Not surprising given what little she knew of him. Well, Huntly could sit atop the coach with the driver and groom, for all she cared. Though, they probably didn't want his company either. Outside of their brief introduction, the only other time she'd seen Huntly had been at the ball hosted by Lady Trent. The same event where she'd assumed Honora would refuse Southwell's attentions and thus spare Emmagene from attending a wedding and house party. At that event, Huntly had stepped on a young lady's dress, carelessly destroying the hem. She'd later seen him stomping around the buffet set up for the guests. He dropped a canapé into the punch bowl.

Huntly reminded her of a shaggy, poorly behaved dog that tracked dirt all over the furniture and slobbered before dropping a duck at his master's feet.

"I am the Earl of Huntly. South's cousin." He waved a giant paw about. "I've been polite. Now you do the same. Trade seats with me."

Rules dictated the gentleman face backward when riding in a coach. Surely Huntly knew that. Even so, had Huntly made the request of her with even an ounce of civility, Emmagene would have been happy to accommodate him. Alas, he had not.

"I don't think so."

Huntly, unbelievably, was still considered to be one of London's most eligible bachelors, largely because he was relatively attractive and hugely wealthy. She supposed if a woman adored a man with a bearlike physique and blatant disregard for anyone's feelings but his own, Huntly might hold *some* appeal. A tiny bit.

Emmagene wasn't one of those young ladies. Nor did she tolerate boorishness, no matter if the gentleman in question was an earl or a day laborer. She picked up her book and proceeded to ignore him as the coach began to once more roll forward.

"I become quite ill sitting backward," he stated again, this time nearly shouting.

"One of your many faults, no doubt," she said without looking up. "And I'm not the least hard of hearing. However, your aversion to sitting in that seat isn't any of my concern. Close your eyes. I'm sure you'll manage." Her dislike of Huntly, weddings, house parties, and indeed her own mother was reaching a fever pitch.

A low hiss escaped him. "I know you, don't I? I never forget a face."

"Forgive me if I doubt you to be that observant."

His eyes narrowed to slits. "Christ, you're Mrs. Culpepper's wizened spinster of a cousin. I suppose that's why Lady Trent found it appropriate to allow us to travel together. There's no worry about damaging *your* reputation. I'm probably the closest a gentleman has got to your skirts in years."

The pads of her fingers bit into the page of her book. She longed to throw it at his head.

He tapped a blunt fingertip to his lips, drawing Emmagene's attention to his mouth, which was rather nice and something she shouldn't notice. "Now let me think. What is your name? It rhymes with bi—"

"Stitch." Emmagene slammed the book shut before he could finish his sentence. "I am Miss Stitch."

The corner of his mouth tilted up, then he stood, rather gracefully for a large man in a moving coach, and peered down at her.

Awareness skimmed down Emmagene's chest and stomach. She was suddenly very cognizant of how small the coach seemed with Huntly in it. She licked her bottom lip out of nervousness.

His eyes tracked the movement before he reached across the small aisle of the coach and gripped her shoulders.

Emmagene squeaked in surprise.

Bodily picking her up, Huntly turned and deposited Emmagene in the seat he'd just vacated. Winking at her, Huntly sat down himself, a smug look of satisfaction on his rough features.

Emmagene's lips parted, as she was so outraged she could barely think.

"Your eyelid is twitching. Are you going to have a fit of apoplexy? Should I have them stop the coach? Maybe drop you somewhere?"

"Drop me?"

He was drumming his fingers on the seat. The digits were thick and blunt. Powerful. Very ungentlemanly without gloves. Something coiled low in Emmagene's midsection as she took in his hands and knew they'd been on her.

"I suppose you're only disappointed I didn't do something

improper. Probably hoping I would. Rest assured, Miss Stitch. Your virtue is safe from me as well as every other gentleman in London. Your reputation precedes you."

"As does yours. I insist you stop this coach and take another. Perhaps your own."

Huntly rolled the mountain of his shoulders. "It isn't available at the moment, which is why I find myself in your delightful company." He pushed himself into the corner so his legs could stretch out over the entire length of the vehicle, or at least as much as possible. Crossing his arms, he closed his eyes. "Don't disturb me."

Emmagene's fingers tightened on her book, anger making the hair on her arms prickle. Huntly's arrogant reputation was well deserved, his boorish manner not exaggerated.

"I can hear you puffing with feminine outrage. Are you up-set," he said in a bored tone, "I referred to you as a spinster? I was merely stating fact. You're clearly a lady of mature years." He opened his eyes. "And unwed." The sharp blue gaze took in her plain brown traveling ensemble. "It wasn't meant as an insult, only a statement of fact."

"Far better than being a foul-smelling oaf with feet the size of a draft horse's."

"I'm not foul smelling." Huntly sniffed at his coat he shrugged. "Maybe a little. Forgot all about this blasted wedding until I arrived home a short time ago. Barely had time for coffee and a bite of breakfast. Look, Miss Stitch." Huntly turned his palms up in a gesture meant to placate her, and it might have, had it been from anyone other than Huntly. "I know the traveling arrangements aren't pleasing for either one of us, but the drive to Longwood is short. Trust me, if I had my own coach, I would be in it."

Which begged the question of the whereabouts of Huntly's coach. "Did you gamble it away, my lord?"

His jaw, in dire need of a shave, hardened in response to her question.

"I understand gentlemen of your caliber are quite prone to offer up their purses for the most ridiculous things." Emmagene leaned forward, catching another whiff of cheap perfume. "You smell like a brothel, by the way."

"How would you know, Miss Stitch," he snarled, "what a brothel smells like? Or even have any idea of what transpires at such an establishment? It isn't the sort of place a lady such as yourself would frequent."

"True, I've never been to a brothel," she said, deliberately leaving the rest of the statement unanswered. "But there is no mistaking the scent of disappointment and poor decisions."

His eyes narrowed into slits before finally shutting completely.

Emmagene opened her book once again and stared down at the page. Her skin was still prickling madly in awareness of the beast across from her, a wholly unwelcome response and one she put down to the unmitigated gall of Huntly. Far more bothersome was the fact that no one, including Southwell's driver and footman, was the least concerned about Emmagene being in Huntly's company for an extended period of time. Especially Huntly.

The knowledge pricked at her. Just a bit.

Shouldn't Lady Trent have objected to her being alone with the Earl of Huntly? Was Emmagene's lack of appeal so assured? Cultivating such a severe demeanor had been necessary ten years ago. Then it had become habit. Now…well, *now* it suited the woman she'd become. Miss Emmagene Stitch, spinster.

She turned her attention back to her unwanted traveling companion, marveling at the sheer size of him. Huntly sucked up all the available air in the coach, infusing what was left with a stale odor from his wanderings the previous night. He probably had been at one of London's gambling hells, women dangling from his muscled forearms. She could picture such a thing in her mind because despite his horrid personality, Huntly wasn't at all *unattractive*, especially when he wasn't speaking.

The bones of his face, Emmagene mused, were all harsh cuts and slashes, as if someone had taken a large piece of granite and hacked away until Huntly had emerged from the stone. There wasn't a hint of refinement about him, which considering he was an earl raised with wealth and privilege, seemed somewhat deliberate on his part. He was rumpled. Unshaven. Ungloved.

Completely ungentlemanly.

His legs, sprawled across the aisle of the coach, were thick with muscle, beneath the fabric of his trousers. The booted feet, even now dropping another clump of mud, were enormous. Her gaze traveled up to his torso, her noting the careless way his cravat was tied, as if he'd done it himself with little thought. Maybe he didn't have a valet, which seemed odd for a man of his station. Probably couldn't find anyone who could tolerate working for him.

Emmagene could barely stand to ride in a coach with Huntly, let alone what a valet must endure. Dressing and undressing him. Trimming his hair.

Again a slow burn of heat suffused the skin of her arms, growing warmer the longer she regarded Huntly. He'd unsettled her in much the same way when they'd first been introduced. Her skin had prickled that time as well. In annoyance. Thankfully, they would be at Longwood by the end of the day.

Emmagene squared her shoulders and put her traveling companion out of her mind. She was made of very stern stuff indeed. Tolerating Huntly for the duration of the journey would be no trouble at all.

HENRY ELDRICK, THE Earl of Huntly, deliberately let out a rumbling snore guaranteed to irritate the starched and pressed woman across from him. She was an incredibly sour, tart thing, with her scowling lips and her tightly braided hair. If only Miss

Stitch smelled of violet water or something equally nauseating, he might have been able to forget her presence.

No such luck.

Miss Stitch, as it happened, smelled of honeysuckle, a decadent and frivolous scent that belonged on a more sparkling and adventuresome young lady.

Her mouth, lips far too plump to belong to such a waspish woman, pursed in annoyance as his snore echoed through the coach. She might try to suffocate him, which would put her slender honeysuckle-smelling body in close proximity to him. He doubted Miss Stitch would ever risk such a thing. She hardly allowed her drab skirts to touch his boots.

Despite the fact she smelled so delicious, there was little else about Miss Stitch to draw any man's attention. She possessed few, if any, curves, though there had been some softness beneath his fingers when he'd picked her up. She was dressed like a wren about to molt for the winter. Had her hair pulled back so tightly from her temples it stretched her eyes into slits. Possessed features that were permanently twisted as if she'd bitten into an unripe plum.

Henry found her *unbelievably* arousing.

He thought the reason might be her ear or, more specifically, the spot where her neck ended at the curve of her ear. She'd taken off her bonnet, and there were small wisps of roasted chestnut hovering at her temples and cheek. Imagining what lay under that ugly traveling dress would make him mad if he allowed it. A vision rose before him, of Miss Stitch with her unbound mass of hair swirling over her shoulders as her mouth, with those plump lips, trailed across his stomach to—

Bloody hell.

Henry had a healthy appetite for women, but even he would look twice at seducing a shriveled prune like Miss Stitch. That he found her so oddly seductive was troublesome. He blamed it on lack of sleep. Most of the previous evening, into the wee hours of the morning, had been spent playing faro with that prick

Halstead, who had intentionally forced Henry into losing his temper.

"Not much like your brother, are you?" Halstead had droned.

"I suppose not," Henry had snarled. "Because he's dead."

Douglas had been dead for some time, but the comparisons to him continued even during a game of cards, as it happened. Henry was nothing like Douglas. If his parents were still alive, the former earl and countess would have spent hours detailing what a disappointment their youngest child had become. The very opposite of their beloved elder son.

Henry shifted in the seat, the familiar wound, never fully healed, opening enough to bleed. It certainly put a damper on his erotic thoughts about Miss Stitch.

CHAPTER TWO

"LADY TRENT, YOU remember my cousin, Miss Stitch." Honora smiled, fingers pressing into Emmagene's arm, a warning to not say anything rude.

Emmagene forced her lips into a smile, dipping stiffly. "Lady Trent." She detested all the bowing and scraping that attached itself to society. Once, Emmagene had thought it would be very fine to have others defer to her when she'd assumed, wrongly of course, that she would become the wife of a lord. In her first season, Emmagene had paid attention to every rule, every bit of society's dictates that must be adhered to. Her manners had been impeccable. In retrospect, it had all been an incredible waste of time and effort, the only person remotely pleased by her adherence to such a strict societal code having been her mother. Emmagene would have been better served learning how to knit, for instance. Or weave. A wrinkle started between her brows as she thought of herself behind a gigantic loom, creating a tapestry with a Greek myth upon it, sipping on a glass of brandy.

"Miss Stitch, is there something wrong?" Lady Trent said, lightly touching her wrist. "You seem troubled."

Emmagene had been troubled the moment she'd seen Lord Huntly in the coach taking her to Longwood this morning but didn't dare tell Lady Trent. Arriving at this house party hadn't bettered her mood. "No, not at all, my lady." She beamed back a bit too brightly.

Honora tensed, shooting Emmagene a glance to mind her tongue.

"I was worried the journey here hadn't been agreeable." Lady Trent frowned, her elegant features made more lovely by supposed worry over Emmagene. "I'm told once the tracks are laid for the rail station, the trip to Longwood will be much quicker, though in this instance, it is of no help. I do hope the coach didn't rock too dreadfully on these country roads. Longwood is *so* isolated. And I *must* apologize for my lapse about Lord Huntly. Truthfully"—she leaned in—"I'd forgotten all about retrieving him from London, but please don't tell South." A conspiratorial wink was thrown in Honora's direction. "Huntly's own coach is being…repaired. I'd hoped it would be available for the trip but received word it would not be. I do hope it wasn't a dreadful inconvenience, Miss Stitch."

She was sorely tempted to slap the kind smile, which she was certain was false, from Lady Trent's lips. Huntly was the very epitome of an inconvenience, as her hostess well knew. "Not at all, my lady. My cousin"—she nodded to Honora—"provided me with a riveting novel for the trip. I barely noticed his presence."

"I know Huntly can be difficult." A curl at her temple batted against her forehead as she spoke. "He's a cousin of South's, though whether on his mother's side or father's side, I can never seem to recall. South has so many relations I fear I can't keep track of them. Huntly, however, tends to stand out as I'm sure you'd agree."

"Our journey together was uneventful," Emmagene assured her.

"Wonderful." There was disappointment in her pleasantry. Lady Trent had probably been hoping Huntly would toss Emmagene out of the coach at some point during the journey. "I was hoping the two of you would get on."

"Well, I wouldn't say we got on, my lady."

But Lady Trent's eyes were already scanning the room behind Emmagene for anyone else she could converse with, like a drowning woman seeking a bit of driftwood to latch onto. This entire polite conversation was for Honora's benefit.

"I hope you've found the rooms I picked out agreeable?"

The rooms Lady Trent had chosen for Emmagene, besides being in a completely different wing from those of the other guests, overlooked a struggling patch of vegetation interlaced with gravel and brick, likely the worst view Longwood had to offer. The mattress was full of lumps, the pillows sparse. She did hope the servants wouldn't forget where she was.

"Very lovely, thank you," Emmagene answered.

"Splendid!" Lady Trent exclaimed with a cluck of her tongue.

At her side, Honora sagged with relief that the exchange had not produced any sort of heated discussion.

Emmagene gave her cousin's fingers a small pat. Though Lady Trent was in dire need of it, she would do nothing to ruffle the feathers of their hostess. Lady Trent had been unfailingly kind to Honora. Partly out of guilt, Emmagene thought, for the role she'd played in the brief estrangement of Southwell and Honora. Still, Lady Trent had not batted an eyelash when Honora had declared her mother would not be assisting in the arrangements, nor would Honora's family, save Emmagene, be part of the house party and wedding. Instead, Lady Trent had stepped in and arranged everything, including attending the fittings for Honora's wedding dress. But the main reason why Emmagene would tolerate Lady Trent was her adamant defense of Honora. When Aunt Agnes, Honora's mother, had tried to pay a call on Lady Trent, she'd been turned away.

Loyalty was something Emmagene admired.

"Oh, I see Lord Carver is here. I wasn't sure he would be able to arrive tonight. Some sort of upset at the museum. Please excuse me, my dear, won't you?" She pressed a quick kiss to Honora's cheek before floating away.

Honora watched Lady Trent, a frown on her lovely face. "I'd no idea, Emmie, that you were stuck with Huntly on the ride here. I should have taken a firmer hand with the details to make sure your rooms were close to mine."

"Your rooms or Southwell's?" Emmagene doubted her cousin spent any time in her own quarters.

"Emmie." Honora shook her head, then laughed softly. "Southwell's, of course. He doesn't care to have us sleep apart," she murmured in a low voice before casting her gaze in Lady Trent's direction. "I allowed her to arrange everything. It isn't something I would have enjoyed, what sort of flowers should be in vases and what the menu should look like. And after what happened, well, I knew it was her way of making things up to me."

"Don't give it another thought. I'm far past the age where a chaperone is required, Honora. I'm certain Lady Trent was aware. I read my book. Huntly snored." Emmagene left out the part where Huntly had bodily moved her across the coach. "It was a wholly uneventful journey."

"Huntly's terrible. Mostly." Honora laughed softly. "Not enough to scare the ladies off completely, but then, he is wealthy and titled. His manners leave much to be desired though. He seems very bent on offending nearly everyone he comes in contact with. A bit too blunt for my tastes, and I am a person who appreciates honesty."

"You don't find him charming like your beloved Southwell?"

"Not in the least. Huntly ogled my bosom the first time we met and didn't bother to hide it. Southwell was quite furious at him. I fear my future husband has the very *worst* taste in friends." She nodded in the direction of Lord Montieth, who was lurking around the room. "Montieth is awful as well. I've had more entertaining conversations with the overstuffed chair in my room."

Emmagene smiled back at her. "I don't doubt it."

"Will you be all right for a moment?" Honora was looking in the direction of the Earl of Southwell, who stood across the room, speaking to Lord Carver. "Southwell is looking for me."

The earl's back was to Honora, cane clutched in one hand

while the other was inconspicuously stretched in Honora's direction.

"Of course." Emmagene nodded with a smile. She wandered over to a far wall and pretended to be engrossed in the painting of a church. Discreetly, she peered at the rest of the guests, most of whom she wasn't acquainted with outside of Lord Carver and the Earl of Montieth.

A distinguished older gentleman stepped into the room and pressed his hand possessively against Lady Trent's waist.

"Lord Trent," came a deep voice from behind Emmagene.

Huntly.

Taking a deep breath, steeling herself for disaster, Emmagene turned to the man at her rear.

He had bathed, if the damp curls around his ears were any indication. And shaved. The scent of stale smoke and cheap perfume that had invaded the coach earlier was gone.

"I was hoping Lady Trent had a lover," Emmagene mused. "Might make this party more interesting."

"Perish the thought," Huntly said. "They're nauseatingly devoted to each other." The blue of his eyes was sharp on her. "I have no idea why Lord Trent married her. I find her to be trying."

"Odd, she has the same opinion of you. Aren't you friends with Montieth?"

"I am. Doesn't mean I like his mother." His gaze roved over Emmagene's perfectly acceptable gown of indigo silk, lingering over the high neckline. "Why are you dressed for a funeral?"

Emmagene struggled to keep her tone polite. "Perhaps you merely can't see well, as the lighting is poor in here—"

"You look like you're in mourning."

"The gown is not black but indigo. A perfectly acceptable color for a woman of my standing to wear to dinner."

"Your standing?" Huntly snorted. "How will you be able to move your arms enough to eat?" He peered at the tight sleeves of her gown. "Though it doesn't look like you eat much to begin with. Probably pick at your food." He raised a brow. "You're wispy."

"Will you please go away? Dampen someone else's evening with your charming personality?" Emmagene took several steps away from Huntly. "Just because you have an opinion doesn't mean you should share it." She didn't want anyone to think they were even remotely acquainted.

"Everyone." Lady Trent clapped her hands. "We'll be dining al fresco this evening. The night is so lovely. Please, let us make our way to the terrace."

Guests began to pair off at Lady Trent's command, knowing without a word being said which gentleman would lead which lady into dinner. Honora and Southwell were arm in arm. He whispered something in her ear that made her blush furiously.

Emmagene looked hopefully in Lord Carver's direction. They'd been introduced once or twice, and thinking him a fine dinner companion, she placed a polite smile on her face.

Lord Carver breezed by her with an elegant older woman on his arm.

One by one, everyone left the drawing room, leaving Emmagene with only Lord Huntly. She clasped her hands, prepared to accept her unwelcome fate. Maybe he would do the decent thing and ignore her as well.

"Come along, Miss Stitch." The low baritone brushed over her skin in a pleasurable way. At least his clothing no longer bore the stains of the wine he'd consumed the night before. He smelled better. That was something.

"Must I?" she asked.

"Unless you wish to take a tray in your room." The big shoulders rolled in such a way that led Emmagene to believe he couldn't have cared less if she went to dinner or not. "We are the only two left, as you can see. Though, your hair is pulled back so tightly it may be impacting your eyesight."

Emmagene bit back the sharp reply hovering at her lips. What did it matter if he escorted her to the terrace? She would leave his side soon enough for her place by Honora. "Very well."

A large elbow hovered in her field of vision.

Reluctantly, Emmagene placed her fingers on his sleeve.

D*AMN*, THIS WAS far worse than Henry had first assumed.

He wanted to kiss her. Tart, sharp-tongued, far-too-thin Miss Stitch.

Miss Stitch was so incredibly restrained, from the top of her tightly coiled hair to the high neckline covering her less than ample bosom. The thought of lifting her dull-colored skirts to taste the wildness she so desperately tried to contain made his mouth water.

Henry had put thoughts of Miss Stitch aside and napped for a great part of their ride to Longwood, assuring himself that the unwanted attraction to her had indeed merely been the result of a sleepless night.

Until she'd exited the carriage upon their arrival. Her skirts, ugly waves of dirt brown, had caught on the door—exposing a trim, delicious ankle. Henry's cock, half-asleep for most of the trip, had suddenly sprung to life. As the damned organ was doing now.

Honeysuckle floated up from her, a sweet, decadent aroma that had no business lingering on the skin of Miss Stitch. Shouldn't she smell of lye or something equally abrasive? A scent that would chafe at his skin like a scrub brush instead of this brilliant tingling along his limbs?

Henry had very particular tastes when it came to women. Generous curves. Slightly bawdy personalities. Full bosoms. Adventuresome between the sheets. Miss Stitch displayed none of those attributes, except for possibly the last one.

Tearing his gaze from what little skin showed above the line of her bodice—because, quite frankly, it was making him mad with desire—Henry focused instead on the delicious scent of roasted meat floating in their direction. He *was* starving but less enthused about eating outside.

"Lady Trent said we'd be eating on the terrace," he said, steering her toward the open doors. "I'll be swatting gnats while I try to enjoy my food."

"I'm not much of an outdoors person either," Miss Stitch agreed with a frown.

Henry had already guessed as much. She didn't seem the sort to go horseback riding or skip through the fields, gathering berries. He pictured her in a dark library, perhaps, presiding over a tray of tea and biscuits while she scratched away at her correspondence. Maybe only in her chemise, licking gently at the tip of her pen as she wrote.

Jesus.

He stared at the curve of her ear. A tendril of her hair had escaped from one tight braid and now lay against the delicate arch, making his hand twitch with the need to touch her. Henry wanted to do things to Miss Stitch with his fingers. His tongue. His mouth. He imagined she tasted like a tart apple.

His trousers were becoming unbelievably tight.

Lady Trent floated about the terrace, directing the guests to one of several tables, their place settings and cut crystal shining in the light of the candles. The front table was instantly filled with Lord Trent, South, Mrs. Culpepper, Montieth, and a young lady who appeared to be dazed at her good fortune of sitting with such esteemed company. Henry recognized her as Miss Cradditch, an annoying young woman on the hunt for a titled husband and the niece of Lady Bainbridge, who was also in attendance.

He wanted to laugh out loud at Montieth's misfortune. At least Miss Stitch was entertaining.

As the other guests found their places, Henry counted the ones being directed to their seats by Lady Trent, who had not once glanced in the direction of him and Miss Stitch. One table, smaller than the rest, stuck out at the edge of the terrace and contained two place settings.

Henry gave a sigh of resignation.

Lady Trent, it appeared, had not forgiven him for the numerous incidents that had occurred at her ball. Henry wondered what Miss Stitch had done to their hostess, for surely the other place setting was for her.

Pointedly dropping her fingers from his arm, Miss Stitch, smug smile in place on her luscious lips, went toward the head table, relieved to be free of his escort.

Henry could have told her not to waste her time, but he didn't. Best Miss Stitch find out on her own. He waited patiently for her to realize her place would not be at the head table but with him.

Lady Trent, catching sight of Miss Stitch, came around the main table, took Miss Stitch's hand, and spoke to her, an apologetic smile fixed firmly on her lips. She turned Miss Stitch toward Henry, doubtless asking for her understanding.

Miss Stitch nodded and walked back the way she'd come. She did not look pleased.

CHAPTER THREE

EMMAGENE MADE HER way across the terrace, back stiff as a board, and cast a glance in her cousin's direction. Honora was so engrossed with Southwell she didn't seem to have any idea her cousin had been banished to the dark depths of the terrace. Emmagene had known of Lady Trent's dislike of her and vowed before even packing to leave for the house party that she would not make a fuss no matter what was thrown her way.

A resigned sigh came from her before she could stop it. She hadn't thought Lady Trent's torture would involve Huntly.

The lighting was so poor Emmagene would barely be able to see what she was eating. Not that she had an appetite. She eyed her dinner companion, difficult to make out in the glow of the candles. Maybe if she didn't look directly at him, Huntly would fade into the shadows.

"Wine. Here." Huntly waved a large paw at a footman.

"So incredibly rude," Emmagene murmured under her breath. She was already far too aware of the presence of his massive bulk so near hers. Huntly could easily be pictured in animal skins, stomping out of a cave with a creature clutched in one meaty fist.

Emmagene shivered. It wasn't nearly as unwelcome a vision as she'd hoped.

"There isn't any reason for you to mumble to yourself, Miss Stitch. In case it has missed your notice, we're seated a great deal away from everyone else."

"Not a great deal. Several feet."

Huntly rolled his eyes. "My point is, feel free to speak your mind. It is doubtful anyone else will hear you, and if I don't care for what you say, I won't listen."

Emmagene regarded him. "I don't wonder that Lady Trent saw fit to seat you here."

"Or you, Miss Stitch. I can't think of any reason"—sarcasm dripped from his words—"you wouldn't be at the main table and basking in Lady Trent's company. Or conversing with Lady Bainbridge and her nitwit niece."

Emmagene's jaw clamped so tightly she might break a tooth. Huntly, damn him, had a valid point. Perhaps Lady Trent's dislike was due to more than Emmagene's treatment of Southwell. Her personality could be exacting to those that didn't know her well.

Come, Emmagene. Your own mother claims you are caustic.

"And, Miss Stitch, if I don't remind this fine young man that we are here"—Huntly gestured to a footman, who looked terrified to have gained the earl's attention—"they'll forget about us."

"I doubt anyone could forget about you, my lord." His personality alone might scar a person after their being exposed for too long. "I'm sure Southwell's staff is very well trained. You only take great delight in being boorish, my lord."

"Boorish?"

"Yes. It means you are poorly mannered. *Coarse.*" She raised her brows to make her point.

"I know what it means, Miss Stitch. I don't need a lesson from you as if you are my governess. Or headmistress of a school." His voice dipped an octave, and Emmagene had the distinct impression of her clothing disappearing under that shocking blue gaze. "You certainly dress like one."

Emmagene's toes, having a mind of their own, curled inside her slippers. "Spoken by a man who sported a large wine stain on his waistcoat just a few hours ago."

Huntly shrugged. "Merely an observation, Miss Stitch. Very alluring, dressing like a two-year widow. I'm shocked you haven't blessed some deserving gentleman with your hand in marriage."

Emmagene snapped her face down toward her plate so quickly she risked hurting her neck. Huntly was…hateful. *Horrid.* Completely reprehensible. What business was it of his how she dressed? She was unwed by choice. The last thing she wished to do was attract any gentleman's attention and have to endure the endless and false declarations of affection.

"If we must tolerate each other's company for dinner, my lord," Emmagene barked, "can we agree to not speak? I believe pheasant is on the menu this evening. A favorite of mine. I would like to enjoy my meal without conversing."

"Overly sensitive, aren't you? It was only an observation, Miss Stitch. Perhaps *that's* why you're sitting here with me and not at the main table. One word uttered improperly might send you to your room."

"Do you cause distress to everyone you meet, my lord? Does it amuse you?" She glanced at the main table. While Emmagene didn't care for Montieth, as Honora's sole family member in attendance, he should have escorted her into dinner and seated her next to her cousin. A large amount of annoyance dusted with anger filled her. Possibly Emmagene wasn't the most likable lady in attendance, but she was Honora's cousin and she certainly didn't deserve to spend dinner with Huntly.

Lady Trent floated effortlessly among the other tables, seeing to the comfort of the guests she actually gave a fig about. Eventually, she made her way toward Emmagene and Huntly, the skirts of her gown brushing against the floor of the terrace with a soft rustle.

"Lord Huntly, Miss Stitch." The apologetic tone greeted Emmagene's ears. "I felt I must come and apologize once again for the seating arrangements tonight. The weather was so fine I thought we should dine al fresco—"

"A splendid idea, my lady," Huntly interrupted.

Lady Trent's lips pursed just slightly, the only sign of her irritation.

Emmagene resisted the urge to elbow Huntly. "I was hoping, my lady, I would be seated next to my cousin. I'm sure you understand."

Another regretful smile graced Lady Trent's lips. "I do, and it is entirely my fault. I can only apologize for my oversight. My sole excuse is that I was working on the seating chart quite late, and I fear I should have worn my spectacles. I mistakenly put Miss Cradditch"—she motioned at the blonde blinking up at Montieth—"instead of you, Miss Stitch. The names are very alike, you see. Now that everyone is seated, I don't wish to cause undue distress by rearranging people while dinner is about to be served."

Emmagene understood perfectly. Miss Cradditch couldn't possibly risk being exposed to Huntly over the course of the meal. An older lady, a spinster, was a far more acceptable dinner companion for him. "Of course, my lady." If she hadn't been subjected to the coach ride with Huntly, Emmagene might have accepted Lady Trent's ridiculous excuse as the truth.

Huntly coughed. She suspected he was laughing at her or the situation. Probably both.

"I am terribly sorry. But at least you and Lord Huntly are previously acquainted from your journey here." Another smile from Lady Trent. "Oh, there's the first course. Excuse me, won't you? I must give instructions to South's butler, Dunst. The staff is woefully inadequate to meet the demands of a house party." Lady Trent nodded and fluttered away in a cloud of silk and roses.

"If the English had Lady Trent at their front lines years ago, we would have defeated Napoleon that much sooner. You don't raise a gentleman of Montieth's ilk without a small bit of ruthlessness. Don't you agree, Miss Stitch?"

Emmagene did, in fact, share Huntly's opinion of Lady Trent, but she refused to give him the satisfaction of telling him so. "I should have made my excuses and taken a tray in my room."

"It isn't too late," Huntly shot back. "I don't mind eating

alone."

"You're such a charming dinner companion I don't imagine you ever indulge in a solitary meal. I'm here." She straightened herself. "I might as well stay."

Huntly held her eyes for a moment. "Brave, aren't you, Miss Stitch? In addition to all your other attributes."

"Courage is overrated." There were times, this moment being one of them, when Emmagene thought she might be better served being an accommodating milksop like Miss Cradditch. Her own bold behavior in the past hadn't exactly benefited her.

Servants arrived on the terrace, pushing carts of covered dishes, and began to circulate among the tables. Huntly watched their progress, narrowing his eyes as he no doubt noticed not one footman had yet to arrive at their table. The wine he'd requested earlier was still absent. Annoyance hovered about his massive shoulders. He shifted in his seat.

"Must you tap your foot so incessantly?" Emmagene tried to remain nonplussed by the lack of attention they were receiving. It would do no good to complain and thus reinforce Lady Trent's opinion of her.

"Yes, Miss Stitch. I must. I'm rather impatient at times." Huntly barely looked at her. "Especially when I'm hungry."

A footman placed a covered plate before him before whipping off the cover with a small flourish.

"Finally," Huntly grumbled.

Emmagene looked down at her own plate, roasted pheasant swimming in some sort of sauce. Taking a small bite, she was unsurprised to find the pheasant lukewarm at best. The potatoes were probably cold. She supposed that made sense, since they were the last served. Nudging one of the peas on her plate, Emmagene cast a glance at Huntly.

He was devouring his food. Methodically. She watched in fascination as first he ate all his pheasant before moving on to the roasted potatoes. Once those were finished, he paused but only to take a sip of his wine before moving to his peas.

"You have a very unusual way of eating, my lord." At least Huntly possessed impeccable manners, which was somewhat of a relief. She'd half expected him to slurp his wine and eat with his fingers.

"How so?" He pierced her with an irritated stare.

"Well, you"—she nodded toward his plate—"seem to avail yourself of only one item on your plate at a time."

The silverware he held over his plate paused at her observation. "A habit I picked up as a child. I didn't think I merited so much of your attention, Miss Stitch, that you would care how I enjoyed my food."

"Perish the thought," she retorted.

"And here I was looking forward to your silence during the meal." The big fingers gracefully moved the knife and fork.

"As you wish." She refocused her attention to the lukewarm potatoes. She would amuse herself by making a list in her mind of all Huntly's unpleasant traits. Arrogant. Rude. Condescending.

"I was a stubborn child," he said abruptly, interrupting her thoughts. "A trial to my parents and nursemaid. A constant source of irritation."

"Having known you only a day, I can agree with that assessment."

Genuine amusement stretched his wide mouth. "You are very prickly, Miss Stitch. I imagine it works wonders under usual circumstances. But you are mistaken in thinking it puts me off."

Emmagene's pulse fluttered unexpectedly from both his words and what was a dazzling smile. Huntly was devastatingly attractive when he chose to be. She immediately pulled her gaze from his to the mound of peas on her plate.

"My nursemaid didn't care for me," he continued in a casual tone. "Which I'm sure you don't find the least unusual either, Miss Stitch. I had difficulty with my letters. Refused to learn to read. I was considered stubborn and not as intellectually gifted as my brother, Douglas. The solution, since I was always hungry, was that I only be permitted to eat what I could spell."

Emmagene watched his features carefully, noting the way the brackets around his mouth sunk deeper as if he was tasting something bitter. His tone would suggest they were only discussing the weather or perhaps something equally mundane.

"Not knowing my letters meant memorizing how to spell specific words incredibly difficult. One word, or sometimes two, was all I could manage at a time."

"Were you served only what you could spell? So—"

"No, my plate was always full of an assortment of things. A way to motivate me, I suppose, or an attempt to broaden my vocabulary. I had to spell out the food, clearly, before being permitted to place it in my mouth. I learned 'tea' first, but it isn't as sustaining as one would imagine. There were days I couldn't spell anything on my plate." He gave her a wry smile.

A rush of empathy filled her for the young lad Huntly had once been. "How old were you?" Emmagene took a sip of her wine. Far too sweet and cloying, much like their hostess.

"Six."

She set her glass down, trying not to show her surprise. An older, possibly more stubborn boy *might* have deserved such drastic measures, but starving a small child was outright cruel. "Your nursemaid should have been dismissed. Didn't you tell your parents?"

Huntly's attention returned to his plate, the man stiffly picking at the pheasant with his fork. "No. It was my mother who suggested taking such a tactic. My brother had set the bar very high, you see. Douglas was quite brilliant." He shot her a wry smile. "And he helped me once he realized what was happening."

"How old was your brother at the time?" she said, quietly appalled. It seemed Honora wasn't the only one with a horrid mother.

"Douglas was eleven."

"He was your *elder* brother? I assumed since *you* are the Earl of Huntly—"

"Dead," he interrupted. "Douglas is dead. I became the heir, much to my parents' enormous disappointment, though neither lived long enough to witness the demise of the earldom they'd predicted would happen were I to become the earl. My ability to finally spell everything on my plate didn't advance their opinion of me. Nor did anything else I accomplished."

Emmagene was familiar with parental disappointment, though her parents would never have done anything quite so cruel. It was obvious the incident had affected much more than the way Huntly attacked his dinner plate.

"Do you have any other questions?" he said in a cool tone.

"I don't believe I do," came Emmagene's curt reply. He didn't want her pity. Nor was she inclined to give it. Poor parents abounded among the wealthy; Huntly wasn't alone in being treated so harshly.

"Surprising. You look the sort who likes to pry."

Emmagene turned back to her plate.

They ate in silence for the next few minutes before Huntly set down his fork with a clatter. He narrowed his eyes at the servants swarming the other tables, jumping about pouring wine and refreshing plates, all while ignoring her and Huntly. With a soft growl, he picked up several peas off her plate with his large fingers and lobbed them at the closest footman, hitting the poor man in the cheek. "I require your service. Now."

Emmagene's mouth popped open in mortification.

The footman rushed over, disconcerted and clearly not sure how to deal with someone like Huntly. "Yes, my lord."

"Pheasant," Huntly demanded. When the man rushed away, he turned to Emmagene. "Close your mouth, Miss Stitch. You don't want one of these tiny bugs or something equally distasteful to fly in." He chucked two more peas at another footman. "I don't like to be ignored, especially under these circumstances. Lady Trent has more than made her point."

The footman slapped at his cheek before turning in Huntly's direction, eyes widening in complete horror that an earl was pelting him with peas.

"Wine." Huntly lifted his goblet and nudged Emmagene. "Did you want some as well?"

"No, my lord." Emmagene bit her lip, trying to stifle her amusement because it would only encourage his continued bad behavior. It was funny, having him hurl peas at a group of footmen because they'd had the audacity to ignore him. He really was just awful.

She glanced away from her dinner companion, gaze landing on Honora. Emmagene's cousin glowed with happiness. Southwell was feeding her a bit of potato, uncaring to anyone who might be watching. Given the earl's history with Honora, was it any wonder Emmagene had had misgivings about their relationship? But even she had to admit Southwell's love for Honora was apparent to anyone who looked at them.

"I don't see the point in marriage, though South is smitten with the Widow Culpepper." Huntly stabbed in Honora and Southwell's direction with his fork. "Don't know why they couldn't just have an understanding of sorts. She is a widow. It isn't as if she's an innocent girl."

"What an incredibly rude and unprincipled comment." Emmagene had once considered the exact same thing. "Why," she'd pleaded with Honora, "must you marry him?" Gentlemen, even those with the best intentions, were bound to eventually lose interest and take a mistress.

Honora had been so bloody angry after Emmagene had voiced her opinion that they hadn't spoken for a week.

Now, tonight, looking over at Southwell and Honora, Emmagene had to acknowledge that love, at least for them, was real. Just because it hadn't been for Emmagene didn't mean she should disparage her cousin for finding such affection. Maybe it was Emmagene who was flawed and unworthy of such an emotion. Wasn't that why she'd made sure never to be enticed by the promise of love again? Because she didn't want to know for sure that she was unlovable?

"Obviously"—she turned toward him—"you have little experience in an affectionate relationship between a man and woman." Huntly's experiences were probably limited to groping his mistress or any desperate woman who found him attractive. Rumor had it there were plenty of those.

A snort. "Because you are, Miss Stitch?" Huntly's gaze raked over her. "Forgive me if I don't assume you to be an authority on the subject."

Dislike for him resurfaced, pushing away every tiny bit of empathy at his spelling story and amusement at his childish actions to gain the attention of the footmen. Did he really believe everyone was entitled to his opinion? Or cared for it? There was a reason Lord Huntly was himself unmarried. Why most of society viewed him as little better than something to be tolerated because he was an earl.

"More so than ill-mannered second sons. At least I've *chosen* not to marry. Affairs are one thing, my lord. Understandings another." Emmagene leaned closer to him, ignoring the way his very presence brushed against her skin. It was annoyance, she supposed. "But affection? It will take all your wealth and your title to compel a young lady into that, I should think."

Huntly's fork and knife hovered over his plate. Possibly he was considering stabbing her with one or both pieces of silverware. "Shrew."

The remainder of the evening would be better spent with a book in her room than trading barbs with Huntly. "Please excuse me, my lord. I fear I've developed a headache." It was a breach of conduct for her to leave the dinner so early, but Emmagene could feel a pounding in her temples, so it wasn't a complete lie.

"It's your hair," Huntly said blandly, returning his attention to his plate. "Pulled far too tight across your scalp. Bound to constrict your mind somehow." He barely lifted himself from his seat as she stood.

She resisted the urge to toss her wine at him.

Emmagene turned and strode to Honora, her excuse for leaving dinner early already on her lips. The journey from

London, she would say, had tired her more than expected. Maybe Huntly would choke on a wedge of potato or a pheasant bone, saving her and the rest of the house party from having to endure his insufferable company.

It was only when Emmagene paused to speak to Honora and Lady Trent that she felt the sting of a pea hitting the back of her head.

CHAPTER FOUR

ENRY KICKED AT a branch blocking the path, gratified when it snapped beneath his foot. He gave it an extra stomp with the heel of his boot. It did not lighten his mood.

Once Miss Stitch had marched off last night in a fit of pique, he'd finished his dinner in blessed peace. There had been no distractions, like the scent of honeysuckle rising from her skin, to keep him from the enjoyment of the wine. Nor the line of her throat, barely visible above the outrageously high neckline of her gown, beckoning him with every turn of her head. Every time she'd moved, Henry had heard the rustle of the silk, more seductive to him than the most generously endowed courtesan. He wasn't sure what had possessed him to mention his family to her. Others had commented on the odd way Henry approached his food, but he hadn't felt compelled to explain a thing to them.

Henry rarely spoke of Douglas. The perfect son and heir. A model gentleman. A true gentleman. He and Douglas had been nothing alike in appearance. Henry had always felt like an oversize giant next to his brother's lean, sinewy build. Douglas wore clothes well. Never went without his gloves. He was well mannered and polite to a fault. Henry's brother had even chosen a perfect, pink-cheeked young lady to be his bride, one with an impeccable bloodline.

Henry, on the other hand, waded through mud and dirt, both as a child and an adult. Laughed loudly. Never felt comfortable in evening clothes. Preferred taverns to the quiet civility of London's gentlemen's clubs. Drank too much. Ate too much. Was careless in his dealings with gentlemen and ladies alike. He would break a young lady such as Douglas had chosen if he wed one. Henry preferred bawdy, experienced women of sturdy build whose tastes in the bedroom wouldn't be quite so delicate.

Henry was still angry at Douglas for falling off that bloody horse and breaking his neck, leaving Henry as the heir and future Earl of Huntly. Henry had been ill prepared for the change in his fortune, nor had he wanted to be an earl. London society had been nearly as stricken as Henry's parents when Douglas had died, leaving Henry to inherit.

Events such as this stupid house party always brought home to Henry how he would never be the gentleman Douglas should have been. He was too big. Awkward. Coarse, as Miss Stitch guessed correctly. His discomfort of society often led Henry to be rudely dismissive before he could be dismissed himself. Lady Trent, in particular, always made Henry uncomfortable. Her dislike of him was well earned.

"How I wish it had been you that mounted that horse."

His mother had whispered those very words to Henry as he'd wept over Douglas. He was sure Miss Stitch would have been in agreement with the Countess of Huntly.

Henry didn't like Miss Stitch, or at least, he didn't think he did, though he did admire her ability to hurl an insult with precision. It was a strange situation, to want to strangle her while also wanting to fuck her senseless. Neither he nor Miss Stitch belonged at a polite house party with a group of people neither of them liked. Her final words, that he would never know affection, pained him because they were true.

She deserved the pea he'd lobbed at the back of her head. He should have added a piece of potato.

Henry looked up into the trees, admiring the stretch of green above his head. This early in the morning, there was still dew on the grass and the surrounding air was filled with the songs of robins and nuthatches. Trees were peaceful beings who didn't care that Henry wasn't Douglas. As were the small sprays of primroses dotting the path. He was well acquainted with these woods, having been lost in them many times when he'd been little more than a child. Longwood was familiar to him. A beloved place. Much more so than Bentwood Park, his father's estate.

Henry could still see his brother standing inside a circle of maple trees, attempting to convince him and South to build a fort. Douglas, aware of his place in the world, had always wanted to take charge of everything as he'd been raised to do. Henry's natural inclination had been to wander off, get himself dirty, and stick frogs in his pockets, knowing it would get him punished. And South? He would wander about with a small leather-bound notebook and pencil, obsessed with mapping out the woods.

A noise came from the thick brush to Henry's right. A deer, most likely. Or a rabbit. Maybe a fox. The woods were full of animals. He paused for a moment, turning slowly in a semicircle, but seeing nothing, he continued on his way. The other guests wouldn't be up and about yet, having lingered in the parlor until well after Henry had retired. Henry would have this narrow path and South's woods to himself until at least midday.

Last night, after Miss Stitch had stomped off and dinner had ended, Henry had joined South, Montieth, and the other gentlemen present for a glass of brandy. He'd behaved himself, mostly. Lord Carver always had something clever to say. Lord Rush, South's closest neighbor, had monopolized most of the conversation by speaking about himself, his enormous white mustache twitching with every tedious word he spoke. Henry had barely listened.

Mr. Harrington and Lord Melrose were expedition cronies of South, which one would think would make them interesting, but they'd been far too immersed in discussing the attributes of an opera singer that one of them, Henry couldn't tell which, wanted to make his mistress.

The other remaining gentlemen were all from London and not memorable, at least not to Henry. Which was just as well, since he had nothing to contribute to any of their conversations. In general, most of those in attendance tended to give him a wide berth, as if he was a wild animal they expected would attack without the slightest provocation. Their opinion had probably been formed after the incident with Lord Stapleton. Stapleton had made the poor choice to remind Henry he wasn't half the man Douglas had been.

"Yes," Henry had said. "But I can throw a punch much better."

He took in a lungful of air before slowly releasing it. Should have stopped at Stapleton's nose, which he'd broken. Montieth had had to pull him off the much smaller man. Unfortunately, Lady Trent may have witnessed the incident.

Miss Stitch had goaded Henry last night. Only, he hadn't wanted to punch her in the nose after she'd dismissed him, not in the least. His plans for her were much more carnal in nature.

The tightening in his groin started again at just thinking of Miss Stitch and her delicious, very un-spinster-like mouth.

He walked a few more feet, mulling over Miss Stitch, and heard a sneeze. Followed by another. Then a string of curses that would have made his drinking companions at the pub blush. A flash of mud-colored skirts, barely noticeable among the deep green of the underbrush, thrashed and spun, drawing his attention.

Henry slowed his steps, eyeing the violently trembling bushes.

"Bloody hell. Let go of me, you damned whoremonger."

Where in God's name had she learned to curse like that? Miss Stitch continued to surprise him.

"Bastard." Another forceful pull bent the top of the bush all the way back. Henry could just make out the top of her head, the sun bringing out the deep-copper highlights in her otherwise dark hair.

Henry cleared his throat, which produced nothing but another furious tugging of her skirts, which he assumed were trapped. He coughed. Loudly. "Miss Stitch."

She whirled around, or as best she could while being entangled by a rather large bush. Trying to straighten and present a more composed front, she failed miserably. The thorns seemed determined to rip the ugly gown right off her slender body.

Henry's cock liked Miss Stitch far more than Henry did. It hardened in his trousers merely at the thought of the spinster stripped of her clothing. Waspish tongue intertwined with his. Or flicking at his ear. Or—

Good God. What *was* wrong with him?

Her eyes widened in horror at the sight of him. She fell to the ground in a pile of brown skirts, thorns tearing at her hem. The first thing Henry noticed, besides the impolite bush, was her hair. Instead of the tortured style he'd become familiar with, Miss Stitch's hair hung in a braid, nearly as thick as Henry's wrist, over one shoulder. The color, a rich chestnut-brown, caught the dappled sunlight streaming through the trees. Greenery, twigs, leaves, and the sort poked out from her hair in odd angles.

Arousal for her struck him, nearly stealing his breath.

"Oh, it's you." Miss Stitch wasn't pleased to see him. Her delectable mouth drew into a scowl, though he sensed a small bit of relief as well that someone had found her even if it was Henry. "How long have you been lurking about?"

"Long enough to know you've a very broad vocabulary for a lady, Miss Stitch. I confess, even my cheeks pinked a bit."

"I can do and say as I please, my lord. I'm far past the age where I would interest anyone, as you have reminded me." She pushed away a stray wisp of hair sticking to her cheek, glaring at him in defiance.

Incorrect. Miss Stitch interested Henry quite a bit, as his cock had not so gently reminded him. "Is that why you've never married? And here I assumed it was only your charming personality."

The mulish tilt of her chin didn't falter. "I assume you're an expert in colorful language. I doubt I offended you."

"I've spent enough time in questionable places to know a few good curse words myself. Haven't used 'whoremonger' in a while though."

Miss Stitch tugged at her skirts to no avail. Defiance lurked in her dark eyes. She didn't want to ask him for help. "Are you enjoying this?"

"Quite possibly, Miss Stitch." He was. Immensely.

Miss Stitch finally gestured to her foot, where a twisting vine covered in small thorns wrapped around the curve of her ankle. "This thornbush—"

"Attacked you without provocation."

"Why must you do that?"

"Do what, Miss Stitch?"

"Finish a person's thoughts by interrupting them?" She gave a small shake of her head, drawing his attention back to the bits of copper in her dark hair. "It's very rude."

"A talent of mine." Sunlight bathed the delicate curve of her ear as he waited for her to ask for help. He was enjoying this far more than he should. His eyes lowered again to the thorny vine clinging to her silk-clad ankle, which was attached to a lovely stretch of well-toned leg, the rest of which remained hidden in her skirts.

Christ. There was an entire expanse of skin beneath the silk stockings just begging for his touch.

She looked away as if something more important than Henry had caught her attention. Finally, a puff of resignation left her, and she turned back to him. "I require assistance to free myself."

"Are you asking for my help, Miss Stitch?"

"I've no other choice."

Henry took a step forward. "May I?" He knelt before she could answer, the honeysuckle of her skin flowing into his nostrils making his cock twitch and his hands unsteady. There was absolutely no reason for him to be so...*enamored* of Miss Stitch.

He enjoyed feminine companionship on a regular basis. Women found him attractive. There was no reason to lust after this woman.

"Unhand me," she said tartly as his fingers neared her ankle.

"Unhand you? I've yet to touch you. Besides, haven't we established that I couldn't possibly find someone of your wizened state attractive? Good Lord. You must be all of twenty-five, possibly twenty-six."

"I'm twenty-eight." She glared at him, as if declaring her age was some sort of gauntlet thrown at him.

"Far too elderly to incite my interest."

Her lips thinned. "Hurry this along."

The pads of his fingers slid over the silk-clad ankle, and he admired the shape of the flesh beneath as he plucked off the burrs. Her calves were well shaped, her legs beautifully curved. Strong. She'd grip him tightly, trapping his hips with her thighs as he thrust into her.

Henry abruptly dropped her ankle with a plop. He retreated into chilly politeness because it seemed that even trading insults with her aroused him. "There you are, Miss Stitch. Good as new." He held out his hand to help her up.

Miss Stitch, true to form, ignored the offer of his hand. She struggled with her tangled skirts, flashing Henry again with her ankles and legs. It took a few moments before she regained her feet with any sort of dignity.

"This is your fault, my lord."

Henry was still thinking of those legs wrapped around him. "I'm not sure how it could be," he replied.

"You were barreling about like some enraged beast, startling me so much I fell into the bush where the thorns caught in my skirts." She furiously brushed the dirt from her dress. A small twig with a bit of leaf still attached managed to stay wedged just above her forehead.

"I didn't realize you possessed such a nervous disposition, Miss Stitch." The leaf beckoned Henry, begging him to touch the silk of her hair.

"Anyone, at thinking themselves alone in the woods and then hearing such a commotion, would have been startled. You could have been a bear. Or a wolf. A band of gypsies—"

"There hasn't been a bear in this part of England in ages. No packs of wolves either. I'm afraid I've no idea about the roaming bands of gypsies."

The little leaf in her hair caught the breeze and fluttered atop the twig.

"The point, my lord, is that I assumed I had the path to myself."

"You aren't on the path, Miss Stitch." He pointed in the direction from which he'd come. "You wandered off it, for reasons known only to yourself."

"It is *very* early in the morning, my lord." She looked down at the ground, as if that explained anything. "Nevertheless, I thank you for your assistance. I am grateful."

"See, that wasn't so difficult. You didn't burst into flames or anything. You are welcome, Miss Stitch." He walked toward the path. "I know the area well if you'd like to continue. Or I can wait here if you prefer and allow you to go ahead of me."

Miss Stitch didn't answer; she seemed to be contemplating her choices. Or Henry.

She jerked her chin, which Henry took as her assent that she meant to continue with him. He started off through the underbrush, back toward the path, listening to the muttered curses as the bramble caught at her skirts. Once they reached the path, Henry shortened his stride to match hers.

"Why don't you wear gloves?" She tilted her chin toward his bare fingers.

No pretense at polite conversation or female twittering as some women were apt to do. "I don't care for them. My fingers grow too warm." The actual reason wasn't something Henry cared to share. The late Earl of Huntly, in one of his wasted attempts to make his younger son into a gentleman, had made

Henry wear his gloves all day and then to bed each night. When his hands had outgrown the leather, his father had forced his hands into the gloves until Henry couldn't even wiggle his fingers. Douglas had eventually convinced their father to relent.

"Why do you braid your hair back so tightly the corners of your eyes are stretched nearly to the back of your head?"

"Not so today." Her fingers brushed against the sole braid dangling over her shoulder. "I suppose I feel a more severe hairstyle complements my appearance."

It did nothing for her appearance, which Henry supposed was the point. Everything about Miss Stitch was designed to keep any male from admiring her. "It's a lovely color, by the way." The words came out as soon as he thought them. "Your hair."

"Thank you." The compliment had made her uncomfortable; he could tell by the way her slender form grew stiff and angled away from him.

They made their way down the narrow trail in companionable silence, her skirts occasionally brushing against his legs. He remained intensely aware of her next to him, his gaze wandering to the braid of her hair as it bounced against her shoulder. A few strands had pulled free, wafting like ribbons in the breeze.

"Did you hit me with a pea last night?" A tiny twitch of her lips followed her question.

"I'm afraid I did, Miss Stitch. I'd hoped you'd appreciate the distance from which I made my shot."

"Indeed, I do, my lord. The main table was…quite a distance from where we were seated." There was a wounded quality to her voice. "We are neither of us well liked, I think."

"Do you care about being thought wonderful by Lady Trent and a bunch of half-wits?"

Miss Stitch nibbled at her plump lower lip. He could see that she *did*, in fact, not care to be disliked in such an obvious manner. A rush of protectiveness toward her filled Henry, mixing with the lust he had for her.

"Outside of Mrs. Culpepper, South, Montieth, and possibly

Lord Carver, the whole lot of them speak of nothing but horses, gowns, the weather, and whatever gossip they've managed to dig up on each other." He looked down on her. "The ladies are even worse."

Her lips pulled into a quiet smile. "You're a bit jaded, I think."

Another hint of honeysuckle lit on his tongue. She must bathe in it.

"I am. I don't mind admitting it. I knew in coming here I might be somewhat unwelcome."

She gave him a thoughtful look. "Then why subject yourself, my lord?"

Henry didn't answer right away, considering how best to reply. Finally, he decided on the truth. "Because of South. We aren't exactly friends just now; the fault is mostly mine."

"No big surprise there."

South and Montieth had once been his friends, but now Henry suspected they merely tolerated him, as one did any unwelcome relation. He'd been walking about telling himself it didn't matter, to be thought of as a boorish, lesser version of Douglas.

"I suppose I wanted to be here when South vowed to love and only bed one woman for the rest of his life. Mrs. Culpepper is a lucky woman. She gets to be a countess." South didn't care whether he left an heir, and he'd often told Henry he had no wish to marry.

"Do you think that's every woman's goal in life, my lord? Marriage? To a title?"

"I do. Which is why I'll have no trouble finding a wife one day, despite your remarks from last night, Miss Stitch."

"I only said you would marry without affection, not that you wouldn't marry at all." Miss Stitch stopped in her tracks. "And in regard to my cousin, Southwell should be on his knees, thanking whatever god he prays to that someone of Honora's caliber would deign to look in his direction, let alone marry him. She is far better than he deserves. Given his former reputation and that of gentlemen in general, it is only a matter of time before he disappoints her. He'll have affairs, I'm sure, and lie to her about them. Gentlemen are expert liars."

Such *vehemence* colored her tone. Even the leaf atop her head trembled in agitation. Miss Stitch didn't have a high opinion of the opposite sex, it seemed; no wonder she worked so hard at keeping gentlemen at bay.

"What would you know of indiscretions, Miss Stitch? Oh, don't tell me. You've had your own."

Miss Stitch turned a brilliant shade of pink.

"No. Surely not." But Henry saw the truth in the darkening of her cheeks. Hadn't he sensed the restraint in Miss Stitch? The thought of her secretly being wanton made the entire lower half of his body tighten with arousal.

"Is it so hard to believe?" she snapped back at him, offended.

"Frankly, yes. Just look at you." Everything about Miss Stitch was designed to repel the opposite sex, from her expensive but unattractive clothing to her sharp tongue and harsh opinions of others.

"You are the most obnoxious human being I have ever met." Her voice raised an octave. "Insulting and condescending at the same time. How dare you disparage my appearance when your own leaves much to be desired. You remind me of a poorly trained dog, slobbering all over his master's guests and stealing food off the table."

"At least I don't resemble a stick with eyes," he growled, angry at desiring a woman with whom he couldn't even have a decent conversation without stooping to insults. "And you've got a leaf in your hair. You look ridiculous."

The light shifted through the thick canopy overhead as they came to the edge of a clearing, softening the sharp angles of her face. Wisps of dark hair played against the line of her neck, drawing attention to the creamy luster of her skin. His desire for her sharpened as swiftly as his annoyance.

She reached up and pulled the offending leaf from her hair. "It is no wonder to me, my lord, why Lady Trent and indeed the rest of the house party avoids you, because—"

Her words were abruptly cut off by Henry's mouth slanting over hers.

The absolute relief at finally touching Miss Stitch sent a hard pulse of blood to his cock. A groan escaped him. Her lips were unbelievably soft. Plush. Perfect. He took the thick braid of her hair and wrapped it around his wrist, pulling her savagely against his chest.

A small sound came from her, not of distress but arousal. Her head tilted back, lips parting beneath his, the touch of her tongue nearly bringing Henry to his knees. He skimmed his hand down the line of her back to settle against her narrow waist, inhaling honeysuckle as he fixed his mouth more fully to hers.

Miss Stitch was no stranger to kissing. In fact, she was quite good at it.

They broke apart, as if both realizing at the same time what was transpiring between them. Staring at each other in shocked silence, neither spoke, the only sound the birds singing in the branches above them.

"Why did you do that?" Miss Stitch blinked in confusion. One trembling finger touched her lips. "What possessed you to do such a thing?" There wasn't anger in her words, something he'd expected. Instead, her fingers trembled with another emotion. Fear. Not of him, exactly. But the kiss. It was written all over her face.

"You wouldn't stop talking," he snapped, irritated with them both.

It was the wrong thing to say. Miss Stitch whirled around, entire body rigid, and walked away from him, skirts swirling about her in distress. She did look like an enraged twig.

"You're going in the wrong direction, by the way!" he yelled after her, unsurprised that she didn't so much as pause in her urgency to flee his presence. "Don't become entangled in another bush." He didn't blame her for fleeing, and it was probably best she did. He'd be tempted to kiss her again or do something far worse. She'd find her way back.

He turned and headed down the path, resolving to keep away from Miss Stitch. The very last thing he needed was to involve himself with such a sour woman. Maybe he should just go back to London.

Then Henry heard her scream.

Chapter Five

EMMAGENE PRESSED HER fingers to her lips as she trudged away, wanting nothing more than to get away from Huntly.

He'd kissed her. *Oh. God.* She'd kissed him back.

Huntly. Horrible, terrible, awful Huntly.

Last night after the disastrous dinner in which she'd had peas launched in her direction and been reminded again of her lack of appeal, Emmagene had gone directly to her room, thankful for a moment alone to collect her thoughts. She'd fallen asleep in a chair before the fire after coaxing one of the maids to bring her a snifter of brandy. Maybe it was the wedding or seeing Honora and Southwell so happy, but for the first time in a very long time, Emmagene had dreamed of Geoffrey.

She didn't often allow herself to think of Lord Anderly's son, the gentleman with whom Emmagene had thought she would spend her life. Geoffrey had been charming. Handsome.

A liar.

In the dream, they'd been making love in the stables, in the same empty stall where they'd often met during her first season. The very spot where she'd lost her virtue.

In a horse's stall. She hadn't even merited a bed. Let alone marriage.

Emmagene hadn't been able to see Geoffrey's face clearly through the haze of the dream, though since she'd been in the stables, in that particular stall, it couldn't have been anyone else.

But his hair had been more tarnished brass than gold. The shoulders much too broad. Still, she'd clung to him as they'd made love. When Emmagene had climaxed in the dream, she'd awoken surprised to find herself alone and in a chair before the fire in an inadequate guest room.

And she didn't think it was Geoffrey she'd imagined.

Sleep had become impossible after that, and she'd spent the better part of the night tossing and turning. Finally, she'd thrust aside the covers, deciding a walk in the early-morning light would clear her mind of such nonsense. Geoffrey wasn't worth a moment of her time. The ease with which he'd convinced her to give him her virtue still surprised Emmagene. She'd believed all his declarations of love and never once wondered why he was meeting her in the stables. She hadn't even questioned why he didn't offer for her properly, because Emmagene had been *intoxicated* with the physical aspects of their relationship. She'd *wanted* to be taken against the rough wall of the stable or bent over a saddle, her face pressed against the leather while Geoffrey thrust inside her. She'd enjoyed it. Craved it. Begged for it.

Desire—or more correctly, lust—Emmagene realized, could make a person blind to everything else.

After the announcement of Geoffrey's betrothal to a bland viscount's daughter, Emmagene's embarrassment at believing he'd loved her and the wanton behavior she'd so eagerly displayed had horrified her.

Far better to remain a spinster than a slave to her baser nature.

So immersed in her thoughts of the past as she'd walked through the woods, Emmagene had failed to pay attention to where she was going. She had walked straight into some sort of bush covered in thorns, which had immediately wrapped around her stockings and caught at her skirts. There were at least ten other gentlemen at this bloody house party and yet the only one walking in the woods when she'd required assistance was Huntly.

He'd kissed her, and she, God help her, had kissed him back.

Over the last ten years, Emmagene had indulged herself a handful of times, mostly out of loneliness and only going so far as kissing. A barrister her father had employed briefly. A widower she'd met walking in the park. But none of those gentlemen, whose names she could no longer recall, had been anything like the Earl of Huntly.

Emmagene shouldn't like Huntly, yet she did. Halting her steps, she reordered her thoughts. It wasn't that she *liked* Huntly, necessarily, but Emmagene desired him.

Which was far worse.

He'd tasted of mint and heat, expertly trailing his tongue along the seam of her mouth, coaxing her lips to part. Once in his arms, Emmagene had ceased to forget everything but the man who'd held her. A low growl had come from his chest when she'd kissed him back, the sound stirring to life a soft throb between her thighs. If she wasn't careful, Emmagene would find herself at his mercy. The most unpleasant earl in all of London. Blunt. Offensive. Not the least interested in affection. There would certainly be no danger of falling in love with him. The very idea was ludicrous.

So what was to stop her from taking him as a lover?

Emmagene stumbled over a tree root at the mere thought. This bloody house party had unhinged her mind to a startling degree if she was considering doing *anything* with Huntly.

The path stretched out before her, curving around a trio of beech trees before ending in a small clearing. An enclosure sat in the tall grass, one built of wood and wire. A tiny house nestled in the corner drew her eye. The area resembled the sort of cage one would keep chickens in, though there weren't any chickens about and the gate to the enclosure was wide open. Odd to find something like this in the middle of the woods. Did gypsies keep animals? If so, where were their wagons? Or perhaps she was about to stumble upon a crazed hermit. But wouldn't Southwell know if there were a strange person living in his woods?

Get ahold of yourself, Emmagene.

Curious, she strode to the edge and peered over the fence, trying to discern if anything was inside. The area seemed to be deserted except for some bits of green that resembled the discarded tops of berries.

A flash of black moved through the grass before brushing against her skirts.

Emmagene jumped back, hand pressed to her throat, then shook her head at being so silly. It was probably only a cat, but regarding the enclosure again, she thought perhaps not. Southwell had traveled extensively to exotic locations all over the world. What if he'd brought some sort of creature back with him? Honora had told her about the anacondas that lived in and around the Amazon. Great snakes that wrapped themselves around their prey, strangling it.

Emmagene took another step back, looking nervously into the grass.

Whatever was here, it had found its way beneath her skirts and was now curling around her ankle. Very much like a snake.

Emmagene screamed. Stumbling backward, she tripped and fell back against a hard stone wall. A warm one that smelled lightly of shaving soap.

"Miss Stitch, whatever is wrong?" Huntly's arm skimmed across her waist before settling her more firmly against the muscled expanse of his chest.

Emmagene's insides contracted in a pleasurable way at his touch. Which she did not want. Pulling herself from his embrace, she pointed at the enclosure. "There's something over there. An animal in the grass. It was under my skirts."

"Of course it's an animal," Huntly scoffed with an irritated roll of his eyes. "We're surrounded by flora and fauna. Isn't that what you expected when strolling in the woods?"

"I'm not talking about a rabbit or a…turtle or something."

"A turtle. We aren't even near a stream."

"I mean," she said through her teeth, "that it could be some sort of exotic animal. Southwell could have brought home a creature from one of his trips." She lifted her gaze to search the trees above them. "One of those large snakes, perhaps. An anaconda."

A bark of laughter came from him. "Even if South was inclined to bring home an anaconda, which he wouldn't be, such a creature probably couldn't survive in England. Certainly not living in some tiny house in the woods." He looked at the enclosure. "You're being ridiculous. Probably a cat."

"A cat? Do you practice that snide tone for hours on end to sound so condescending?" She nodded again in the direction of the enclosure. "Not so much as a warning sign to announce there is a dangerous creature on the loose. It's very irresponsible of Southwell."

"I doubt whatever lives here is anything dangerous. But I'll walk around this fence and take a look if it will make you feel better."

"It will."

"You know, Miss Stitch. If you wanted me to escort you back to the house, there wasn't any need to make up a story of a strange animal lurking about in order to get me to do so." He circled the enclosure, moving slowly and looking at the ground.

Emmagene bristled. "I hope it bites you."

The grass rustled just to the left of the fence, drawing their attention. Huntly raised a brow. "Are you sure it isn't some sort of unusual bird?"

"How would I know?" She followed and watched from a few feet away. "He's your cousin."

"I don't see any feathers on the ground though. Or anything resembling a nest. I suppose that's what the house is for."

A black-and-white ball of fur streaked across the grass, in Huntly's direction. She couldn't see it clearly, of course, but it appeared to be vicious. "My lord, perhaps we should leave whatever it is undisturbed."

But Huntly had slowed his steps to approach a quivering patch of grass. "Come now, I won't hurt you," he crooned in his rough voice to something at his feet.

A tingle ran between Emmagene's thighs at the soft, coaxing rumble of his voice. For only a moment, she imagined he was talking to her. Which of course he wasn't. He was talking to whatever was creeping about in Southwell's woods.

"What the bloody hell are you?" she heard Huntly say right before the most appalling, rank odor filled the air. "No, stop!" he yelped, jumping up into the air, backing away as fast as he could in Emmagene's direction.

A small rodent-like animal with a fanned tail and a white streak down its back scurried away into the undergrowth and disappeared. The most noxious stench hung over the entire area, like a gigantic cloud of rottenness.

Huntly moved forward, the cloud of stink firmly fixed to him.

Emmagene held up a hand to stop him. "That's close enough, my lord."

Huntly gave her a wide-eyed look before sniffing at his coat. "Good God. What horrible creature do you think that was? Certainly not a cat. Very unlike anything else I've ever seen. It *sprayed* me."

She pinched her nose. "I've no idea what it is." Waving a hand to dispel the scent, she backed up further. "Oh, it's quite horrid." Emmagene bit her lip to keep from giggling at the look of shock on Huntly's face. "Sprayed you?"

"There's no need to repeat me. Yes, it"—he thrust a large forefinger in the direction of the grass—"sprayed me." Stepping forward, he winced as a breeze blew the smell into his nose. "Christ. The thing pointed its *ass* at me. Wiggled its tail. *Sprayed* me. Now I stink to high heaven."

"You certainly do." Emmagene waved her hand in the air, hoping to dispel some of the scent. "Just don't get too close." A snort followed by muffled laughter came from her as she gave up her struggle to contain her amusement. "Walk behind me. Please, I beg you, my lord."

A grunt of displeasure was the only reply.

After half an hour—in which Huntly took off his coat, sniffed, and then flung the garment onto a tree stump in disgust—of marching back to the house, the odor hadn't abated. He cursed loudly, uncaring that Emmagene heard every word. "The smell isn't going away."

"No, my lord. It is not." Another giggle left her.

"Looked like a cat, but no feline has ever pointed their ass at me and shot such a stench in the air. Stop laughing," he growled as his gaze fell to her mouth. "No, don't. It's a lovely sound even if it's at my expense. You should make it more often, Miss Stitch."

"I'll consider doing so."

"I suppose Lady Trent will use this as an excuse to set a table for me on the other side of the estate." He pushed back the tangle of his hair, frowning as he caught a whiff of himself. "I smell as if I've been mucking out the stables."

The sun lit along Huntly's hair, the mop of tarnished gold atop his head sparkling, and Emmagene found herself glancing anywhere but at him. It definitely hadn't been Geoffrey she'd dreamed of last night.

"Stay downwind of me, if you don't mind, my lord." Emmagene quickened her steps.

The garden came into view as the path gently wound out of the woods and onto the lawn. There was no sign of the other guests or any indication anyone else was out taking an early-morning walk. A good thing considering Huntly's smell.

"Find Southwell's butler, Dunst. He'll know what to do to sneak me back upstairs. I don't want to be responsible for anyone not enjoying their eggs this morning."

Emmagene nodded, for once not arguing, and hurried toward the terrace. Once inside, she searched the corridor for Dunst, finding him directing servants, who were rushing about preparing to serve breakfast.

Dunst was an interesting choice for a butler, as with his build and somewhat menacing demeanor, he looked more suited for employ as a dockworker. Perhaps that was why Southwell had chosen him, for he could certainly frighten off anyone who might not belong at Longwood. She approached him, discreetly relaying the predicament Lord Huntly found himself in.

Dunst's mustache twitched in alarm, but he displayed not an ounce of surprise at the description of the hideous creature. "Most unfortunate." After making some whispered instructions to the head footman, the butler followed her out of the house, to the gardens.

Huntly was attempting to hide beneath a spray of wisteria. Not only was he clearly visible, but the fragrant blooms did nothing to mask the scent. He immediately launched into a description of the horrid creature for Dunst, complete with Emmagene's screams for aid. "It was some sort of—"

"Rodent," Emmagene finished. "Or a very ugly cat possibly."

"Neither, I'm afraid." Dunst shook his head. "It was Peony."

Emmagene exchanged a look with Huntly. "The creature who released such a noxious odor is named after a flower?"

"Peony is *her* name. An ironic choice, I agree. His Lordship finds it amusing. The smell is Peony's way of protecting herself. She only does such a thing when she's very frightened. Or at least, according to Lord Southwell." He gave Huntly a pointed look.

"Don't glower at me like that, Dunst." Huntly crossed his arms across his chest. "You act as if I got down on all fours and insulted it. Her. Peony."

The butler cleared his throat.

"But *what* is she?" Emmagene asked.

"Peony is a skunk and, as far as I'm aware, the only one in England. Lord Southwell adopted Peony while on one of his trips to America. She was orphaned, poor little thing. Very tiny. His lordship couldn't bear to leave her to fend for herself, so he brought her home. Peony has an enclosure." He gave another pointed look at Huntly. "Which you must have invaded, my lord. And she felt threatened."

"Threatened?" Huntly said curtly. "She owes me a bloody

coat at the very least, Dunst. I had to leave mine in the woods due to the stench."

Dunst pinched his nose. "Apologies, my lord."

"Does she"—Emmagene looked at Huntly, trying not to breathe in the smell—"do this often?"

"No, Miss Stitch. Peony has only done so a handful of times. We find vinegar helps get rid of the smell, somewhat."

"Somewhat?" Huntly snapped.

"My lord, you will require a bath immediately. Several of them. Your clothing burned—"

"Burned?"

"The smell—unfortunately, my lord—will never come out of your clothes. Best to burn them."

Emmagene covered her mouth but not quick enough to stifle the snort of amusement coming from her.

Huntly glared at her. "This is your fault."

"If you would"—Dunst kept his nose pinched—"please come this way, my lord, and up the back stairs. We don't want the other guests exposed. Jonas," he barked.

A young lad came running from inside the house before coming to a screeching halt when he caught a whiff of Huntly.

"Ooh." Jonas waved his hand before his eyes widened at seeing Emmagene. "I mean, oh dear, miss."

Another snort escaped her. This was like watching a dreadful play at the theater unfold.

"Peony has claimed another victim, Jonas," Dunst explained unnecessarily. "Please have a bath drawn for Lord Huntly. We'll need vinegar. Lots of soap. I'm afraid you won't be able to dine with the others this evening, my lord, so I'll arrange for a tray to be sent to your room."

Huntly stomped by Emmagene, fists clenched, reeking like a pile of spoiled garbage, while her shoulders shook with laughter. "Not another word, Miss Stitch."

CHAPTER SIX

EMMAGENE SIPPED HER brandy, ignoring the reproving looks of several of the other ladies in attendance. Lady Trent appeared especially distressed Emmagene wasn't calmly sipping ratafia or sherry. Her hostess kept casting her side glances as if waiting for Emmagene to do or say something offensive.

Actually, most of the guests paid Emmagene little attention, as they were too focused on the objects that filled the room. Southwell had created his own museum, so to speak, decorating what was once Longwood's massive ballroom with items brought home from his travels. Emmagene sipped at her glass and took in the wall before her. A hideous mask, lips drawn into an ugly grimace, hung above her. Directly below the mask was a podium on which a pipe, decorated with feathers and beads, sat enclosed in glass.

Emmagene peered up at the mask. The expression was similar to the one Montieth had worn as he was seated next to her at dinner this evening. After having wanted to be escorted by the earl, mainly to be included in the group surrounding Honora, Emmagene had found Montieth as a dinner companion to be boring, at best. He'd been coldly polite, so much so that Emmagene had found herself missing Huntly's abrasive presence. There was only so much conversation one could make about the weather. There hadn't been any peas to be thrown, and Montieth hadn't even addressed any of the footmen directly.

"I understand you met Peony today while out walking in the woods with Hunt." The Earl of Southwell appeared beside Emmagene, a half smile on his mouth, deepening the dimple in his cheek. The earl was a blindingly handsome man with a commanding presence and a wealth of effortless charm. Had she been any other woman, Emmagene would have been dazzled.

"I wasn't walking with Lord Huntly, my lord," she snipped.

Southwell raised a brow at her tone but merely took another sip of his own drink.

Emmagene had the impression he was amused by her, which only made her dislike him more. "We came upon each other accidentally, having both gone for an early-morning walk. But yes, my lord, we did meet Peony. I fear she liked me slightly more than Lord Huntly."

Southwell bestowed a brilliant smile meant to disarm any woman within an inch of him. She suspected it worked more often than not. "Poor Hunt. He must have frightened Peony. She usually doesn't react so strongly. The smell is how she protects herself. Skunks are fairly common in America, which is where I found her."

Emmagene took another swallow of brandy. If Southwell was surprised by her choice of spirits, he didn't show it. "And how did you make the acquaintance of Peony, my lord, if I may ask?"

"I was camping at the edge of a vast forest with my traveling companions. She must have crawled into my tent as I slept. I awoke to find her curled up beneath my chin, barely bigger than my hand. She was quite helpless." He shrugged. "Without the rest of her family, she would be left to survive alone, possibly to be eaten by a larger animal. Our guide warned me what Peony could do, but she's never once lifted her tail in my direction. Only two of my dogs' and a groom's. Oh, and there was a dockworker when I returned to England. He wasn't gentle with her cage."

"And no one else?" Emmagene found it hard to believe.

"I suppose someone might have come across her in the woods and received the same treatment as Hunt, but if they have,

I'm unaware. The trick, you see, is strawberries."

"Strawberries?"

"I feed Peony strawberries." He winked. "She loves them."

Southwell really was spectacular. No wonder Honora was mad about him. "Will Lord Huntly be able to get the smell from his…person?"

"Eventually. The vinegar helps. Somewhat. He should be less odorous tomorrow, but it will take at minimum a day or two." Southwell regarded her closely. "At least you are free of his company tonight."

"No, instead I had to endure Montieth," Emmagene snapped back without thinking. "Of the two, Montieth is more tolerable but barely."

"Agreed." Southwell gave a soft laugh. "Hunt is often far too blunt for his own good and offers opinions best left to himself. But I suppose he comes by some of his bad behavior honestly." Southwell lifted his cane to her before lowering it to the ground again. "We are all the sum of our experiences, Miss Stitch. Hunt is no different."

Emmagene recalled the story Huntly had told her about being made to spell his food. Part of her wanted to ask Southwell about Huntly's family, but she thought better of it. Her question would imply interest in the boorish earl.

"And did your experiences make you a better man, my lord?" Honora had related the tale of Southwell's attack by a black caiman in South America, responsible for the destruction of his left leg and his need for a cane. She claimed it had changed Southwell.

"God, I hope so." He gave her a pointed look. "I'm aware of your opinion of me, Miss Stitch.

"Richly deserved," Emmagene shot back a bit too loudly.

Several pairs of eyes turned in their direction, including Honora's. A concerned look crossed her pretty face. Not for Emmagene but for Southwell.

"You're hard, Emmagene," her mother's voice whispered.

"Again, I must agree with you." Southwell nodded politely, not the least concerned with Emmagene's opinion of him. "Enjoy your evening." He limped his way over to her cousin, the cane echoing against the marble floor. When he reached Honora, their fingers immediately laced together before being hidden in the folds of her cousin's skirts.

Emmagene finished the brandy in one swallow. The conversation with Southwell had left her with an unwelcome sensation in her stomach, as if she'd eaten something spoiled. His observations about Huntly could just have easily been about her.

She glanced at her cousin again. Honora fairly glowed with happiness, her face shining more brightly than the chandelier hanging from the ceiling. Did Honora have to make excuses for Emmagene's behavior?

The troubling thought stayed with Emmagene as she left the ballroom, having lost what little taste she had for pleasant conversation.

CHAPTER SEVEN

AN UNPLEASANT ODOR hung in the early-evening air, billowing around Henry like a cloud.

He grimaced. The scent of vinegar was only slightly less repellent than that of Peony, which still hadn't dissipated completely but was much reduced.

Henry had spent the remainder of yesterday and most of today exactly as Dunst had predicted, sitting neck deep in a succession of baths attended by a footman who appeared at regular intervals to change out the water. Bowls of vinegar sat around his room, which Dunst had told him would help dispel the skunk odor. So much vinegar. Henry was certain he'd never again be able to taste anything else again.

Especially Miss Emmagene Stitch.

While lying in his bed after the last of his vinegar-soaked baths, Henry, cock in hand, had thought of all the ways in which he wanted to debauch Miss Stitch. There were literally dozens. Twice he'd brought himself to release imagining her hair trickling over his stomach and thighs. Her scowling lips on his cock as she sucked him into her mouth.

Christ.

Henry pushed his lascivious thoughts aside, focusing instead on trudging up the slight incline of the small hill at the end of South's lawn. He'd been put at the very end of the line of guests Lady Trent had assembled, without even a servant to watch his back. One well-dressed twit in a powder-blue gown, whose name Henry forgot moments after being introduced, had claimed her eyes were watering at the aroma surrounding the Earl of Huntly.

Henry had been asked, politely, to wait until most of the guests had started up the hill.

Glancing up at the line of torches and servants in a semicircle at the top, Henry knew in his bones he would despise everything about this evening. Their bloody hostess couldn't just have another lovely dinner, one properly seated at South's long mahogany table. Not that Henry, given his smell, would have been permitted to be seated in the dining room. Maybe in the hall. Or possibly Lady Trent could have arranged a boring but tolerable game of charades where Henry could just sip on a whiskey and pretend to be interested.

No, tonight the entire house party had been forced to walk up to the very top of this peak that Lady Trent had decreed the perfect spot from which to view fireworks.

Fireworks. Henry didn't find exploding objects to be interesting or fun in the least.

Arriving at the top of the hill, Henry was unsurprised to find a footman apologetically directing him to a blanket set apart from the rest of the main group. While most of the party was situated toward the front, where the incline sloped in a gentle roll toward Longwood, Henry's blanket was some distance behind the others. *His* blanket backed up to the other side of the hill, a steeply wooded incline ending in a ravine from which he could hear the distant sound of water bubbling merrily along. He'd caught frogs in that stream as a child. Probably rolled down the hill as well, and had no desire to repeat the experience. A collection of large stones edged the water along with quite a bit of the same thorny bushes he'd rescued Miss Stitch from yesterday. Henry couldn't remember what they were called, but he did remember the bruises and scratches he'd received.

If he had too much to drink, one stumble would send him headlong down the ravine. No one would notice. Perhaps that had been Lady Trent's plan all along. The woman was much more devious than anyone gave her credit for.

His hostess, holding a gloved hand to her nose, floated by with an apology in her eyes.

Henry scowled at Lady Trent and turned to settle himself on the blanket, discreetly searching the crowd of guests for a too thin form with tightly braided hair.

"Don't lean back too far. Can't have you rolling down the hill like some giant boulder and ruining the evening." South appeared a few steps away, his voice floating to Henry in the quiet late-evening air. "We won't be able to hear the splash from up here when you hit the stream. I thought I had mentioned Peony to you before."

"You did not," Henry groused back. "I would have remembered an odorous rodent on your property that you were keeping as a pet. And you owe me a new coat." He shook his head. "I should have stayed in London."

South chuckled. "But you would have missed all the fun." Waving his hand about, he said, "You do smell like a large vat of pickled herring. Or something else equally…biting."

"If you're done gloating—"

"I wouldn't call it gloating, exactly, Hunt. I'm merely jealous because you're spared having to socialize." He looked over his shoulder at the other guests. "I don't care for house parties."

"Yes, but Lady Trent does. Where is the lovely Mrs. Culpepper?"

"In that group somewhere." South waved his hand again. "Probably drawn into conversations she doesn't care to have. With Lady Bainbridge in particular. Honora, as you can imagine, doesn't care much for society despite Lady Trent's best efforts. She has that in common with Miss Stitch."

Henry's fingers pressed into the blanket at the mention of the woman who'd been haunting his thoughts. He'd finally decided to give up trying to figure out why.

"She'll find me. Honora, that is. Not Miss Stitch. She's just as likely to take my cane and push me down the hill with her foot." South carefully lowered himself to the ground.

"Hasn't warmed up to you, has she?" Henry knew full well Miss Stitch didn't like South.

"No. Has she warmed to you?" A half smile crossed South's lips as he reached into his coat, producing a small flask from a pocket.

Henry didn't bother to respond to South's comment. The idea of Miss Stitch ever warming to anyone was rather absurd.

"The wine will be around in a minute." South held up the flask. "But I thought you might like some of this. Consider it an apology and a better welcome than you've received thus far."

Henry took the flask, some of the tension leaving his body at his cousin's genuine regret. Opening the top, he sniffed, a grin spreading across his face in pleasure. "Laramie? I didn't think there was any left."

Laramie, a superbly blended whiskey from some tiny village in Scotland, had ceased being produced when Henry and South had still been little more than lads. South's father had had a limited number of bottles, all of which Henry had assumed were long gone.

"We didn't drink all the bottles my father purchased. Some survived. I'd forgotten until Honora took to exploring part of the wine cellar one day." A smile crossed his lips. "She's quite intrepid. Doesn't care for spiders though. They tend to get stuck in her hair." He made a circular motion with his fingers. "In the curls."

Henry took a sip of the caramel-scented liquid, letting the whiskey burn all the way into his belly, thinking of Honora dancing about with spiders stuck in the mass of curls atop her head. "Christ, it's better than I remember." He held out the flask to South.

"Keep it." South patted the other side of his coat. "I've my own. I hope it takes the sting out of your current situation if not the smell. And it may help if you are subjected to Miss Stitch again. I know she isn't...pleasant."

"Something we have in common." Henry looked over at South before taking another sip of the whiskey. "Unpleasantness."

Lady Trent had probably protested strongly to Henry's presence at this house party, but South must have insisted he be here. It was something Henry hadn't really thought about, at least not until arriving at Longwood. He'd been too busy trying to be the worst earl in London and succeeding magnificently.

Henry had considered more than the delightful Miss Stitch while soaking in his vinegar baths. There had been little else to do but review the actions that had led him to be banished to the end of the terrace during dinner.

"Thank you for inviting me, Gideon. For what it's worth, I wish you every happiness."

"It is worth quite a bit, Henry."

They both held up their flasks and drank deeply of the Laramie. The previous Earl of Southwell had been furious when he'd found his finest and most expensive whiskey in the hands of two young lads. Henry had been sent back to his own parents in disgrace. Nothing new.

Mrs. Culpepper, fetching in a gown of vibrant green the same color as her eyes, strolled in their direction, a glass of wine dangling from her hand.

South turned at her approach and stretched out his hand. "Hello, my love."

"Are you hiding, my lord?" She lifted a dark brow. "It seems tales of your bravery might be exaggerated. I'm terribly disappointed." She took South's hand, lowering herself gracefully to the blanket and settling her skirts around her while simultaneously holding her wine. She didn't spill one drop.

Henry was duly impressed.

"A smart man knows when to retreat," South replied. "Do we really know all these people? Because I'm not sure I like most of them."

"I don't believe *we* do," she smiled back. "But Lady Trent

does. You can't imagine I actually requested the presence of Lady Bainbridge and her niece? They are obviously here for Montieth's benefit, though I can't imagine he'd seriously consider Miss Cradditch as a potential bride." Sniffing the air delicately, she turned to Henry. "Lord Huntly, I've been informed of your mishap."

"I believe everyone has, Mrs. Culpepper. South claims he isn't gloating. Are you?"

"Me? Never." A sly smile crossed her lips. "Though, I will admit to offering Peony an extra helping of strawberries. I may have fed them to her by hand."

Henry and Mrs. Culpepper—*Honora*—had a somewhat contentious relationship. He'd insulted her at their first introduction, possibly admiring her bosom longer than he should have, and who could blame him? Her bosom was magnificent. South hadn't been amused, nor had Honora.

"Having an animal do your dirty work? For shame, Mrs. Culpepper."

"I'm quite cunning when necessary, my lord." She took a sip of her wine while South gazed at her in adoration. While Henry couldn't quite conceive why South would want to chain himself to one woman for the rest of his life, he could certainly see Honora's appeal. Petite and voluptuous, Honora was a stunning woman with her raven hair and sparkling green eyes.

He probably *had* stared too long at her bosom when they'd first met. It would be difficult for any man to *not* look in her direction.

"I do not doubt it," Henry replied, taking yet another swallow of whiskey. He was considering how he could convince his cousin to part with at least one bottle of the Laramie when a flash of gray appeared behind Honora.

Miss Stitch. Warmth immediately curled around Henry's legs and up his thighs.

Clad in a gown of pewter, which he supposed was an improvement over the muddy shades of brown she usually seemed to favor, Miss Stitch came closer. Enough so that he could see her hair was bound into a delicate chignon at the base of her neck and not a complicated twist of braids.

Not voluptuous. Far too thin. Meager bosom. Hostile personality.

Henry wanted Emmagene Stitch to the point of desperation.

"Emmie." Honora looked at her cousin in confusion. "I thought you were going to wait for me on our blanket."

Emmie. A girlish nickname for such a prickly woman. Henry meant to address her as such at his first opportunity if only to annoy her.

"Miss Cradditch wouldn't shut up about a trip to her modiste and a striped tulle gown she was having made for a ball for Lord Something or Other." Miss Stitch rolled her eyes. "I was afraid I would fall asleep from sheer boredom and begin to snore thus ruining my determination to remain polite for the duration of the evening."

Jesus. Henry wanted to kiss Miss Stitch—*Emmie*—until all that scathing hostility was channeled into the passion he sensed lurking just beneath her skin.

"She is a bit frivolous," Honora said, standing. "I think she chatters so much because she's terrified of Montieth. I'm not sure what Lady Trent was thinking in throwing the two of them together." The reluctance to return to the rest of the party was clear in her voice. "I'll make sure the servants attend you promptly, Lord Huntly, despite your being on your own island, as it were."

South came slowly to his own feet, using the cane for balance.

Honora immediately took his arm, holding steady until she was assured he had his footing.

Honora, despite her faults, was hugely protective of South, a man who had fought through jungles and been attacked by wild animals. Henry found that oddly endearing.

"Very kind of you, Mrs. Culpepper," he said to her before turning. "Good evening, Miss Stitch." Had Miss Stitch informed her cousin of the poor treatment she and Henry had received the other night? He thought she had.

"Lord Huntly." Her nose wrinkled.

"Are you coming, Emmie?" Honora looked at Miss Stitch, who hadn't taken her eyes from Henry.

Something pulsed in the air between Henry and Miss Stitch, a feeling born perhaps of the unexpected kiss they'd shared in the woods the previous day.

"I think I'll share Lord Huntly's blanket; after all, the cause of his unfortunate accident was due in part to his rescuing me from Peony." The way her lips pursed so delicately as she spoke set Henry's blood racing.

Honora nodded, her eyes flashing between Henry and Miss Stitch. She stopped one of the servants bustling about, the young man leaning down and nodding at her instruction. Montieth soon came upon them, the doll-like Miss Cradditch having vacated the blanket Miss Stitch must have left her on, to cling to his arm. The girl did look mildly terrified. Shocked, perhaps, that she'd gained the attention of Montieth. He was terribly imposing, after all.

"Something amuses you, my lord?" Miss Stitch noted the direction of Henry's gaze.

"Looks like he's dragging about a porcelain doll, the sort his daughter favors for her tea parties."

"Unkind, my lord. Though I do think Miss Cradditch was relieved when Montieth escorted me to dinner last night and she was spared having to make conversation with him. I'm sure there are only so many things her little mind can conceive of to say."

"Now who is being unkind?"

"Me. Do you mind?" She nodded at the blanket. Without waiting for his reply, Miss Stitch abruptly dropped herself, stilted and awkward, at the corner of the blanket and nearly spilled the wine she held all over him. Not at all graceful.

He'd never wanted a woman so much.

"I think I'll sit with you," she said tartly. "No one else here is the least bit interesting."

EMMAGENE, AFTER SETTLING herself on the blanket, with Lord Huntly mere inches away, considered she might have lost her wits.

The smell of vinegar floated on the breeze, the source of the aroma directly before her. Not nearly as bad as the horrible stench of Peony, thankfully, but still enough to make one's nose wrinkle. The hard part was admitting to herself that Huntly *was* the most interesting person at this house party. At least, for Emmagene. Yes, she found him infuriating and rude, but that was much preferable to the cloying annoyance she felt while sitting with Lady Trent, Lady Bainbridge, and that dimwit Miss Cradditch. If nothing else, Emmagene could speak her mind around Huntly. If he didn't care for her opinions, he would tell her so.

"I've been called many things, Miss Stitch. Interesting is perhaps the kindest." The corners of his eyes crinkled at her. He was holding a small flask and took a long swallow.

Emmagene watched the movement of his throat, noting that some sort of effort had been made with his cravat this evening. The effect was ruined by his waistcoat, which was wrinkled and missing a button. No gloves. No hat. Did he even possess a valet?

She finished the remainder of her wine and set the glass down on the blanket. "Aren't you going to offer me"—she nodded in the direction of the flask—"any of that?"

"I don't wish to offend your tender sensibilities." The corner of his mouth ticked up. "Miss Stitch," he addressed her with a low purr.

Emmagene's heart, quiet for so many years, stretched softly in the confines of her chest. "It's far too late for that, my lord. You've long since offended every sensibility I've ever had."

He leaned forward, teeth flashing as he gave her a wicked smile, the flask in his hand.

Now that she'd grown accustomed to the smell, the vinegar wasn't so bad. Certainly tolerable. Lady Trent had only been looking for another excuse to keep Huntly from the rest of the party.

"What did you do, exactly, to make an enemy of Lady Trent?" Emmagene thought of the ball where Huntly had torn a woman's skirts, spilled wine, and generally made a nuisance of himself.

"I think you know, Miss Stitch. You were there that night as well."

Emmagene's fingers stilled on the flask as she felt her heart reach in his direction. "Lady Trent's ball."

"Not my first offense and unlikely to be my last. I had too much to drink. Pissed off South and Montieth. Lost at cards. Took a bottle of wine from one of the servants, then dropped it accidentally. Stepped on a young lady's skirts, ripping the hem. Lady Trent was quite incensed. I suppose she wished me to drop to my knees and stitch the wailing girl's gown back up."

That amused Emmagene. The thought of Huntly on his knees, sewing. Or possibly it was the thought of him on his knees. Before her. His mouth—

The air grew much warmer. Emmagene fanned herself.

"I would like to say," Huntly continued, "that I had never behaved so badly before, but the truth is I had been cutting quite a swathe through society. And not in a way that makes young ladies swoon." His chin tilted toward her. "A small sip, Miss Stitch."

Emmagene considered his words, raising the flask to her lips. "Why?"

"I don't want you coughing and choking. I'd be forced to thump you on the back. The whiskey is expensive and shouldn't be wasted."

"Don't be obtuse; you know exactly what I meant," she retorted. The scent of a very fine blend of whiskey wafted up her nostrils as she took a healthy swallow, shivering when the smoky warmth hit her belly.

His big fingers plucked at the blanket. "Because poor behavior is all anyone has ever thought me capable of, and I don't wish to disappoint them."

Emmagene thought that a very telling and *honest* bit of speech.

"You are a surprise, Miss Stitch."

Huntly's eyes on her were heated, for lack of a better word. Lustful, if she was being truthful. It had been years since she'd had such a look directed at her. Not since she'd been barely eighteen and so foolish. She'd missed the sensation. A delicate, insistent ache began between her thighs, one that had never really faded since their kiss in the woods.

"In what way?" She handed the flask back to him, trying to keep her fingers from trembling. She had a sudden, very real urge to touch him.

"In all ways," he said quietly before taking another swallow of the whiskey. He handed the flask back to her once more, eyes intent as Emmagene took another large swallow.

"Where did you learn to appreciate whiskey?" There was a husky quality to his words that sent pulses of heat around the lower half of her body.

The whiskey, very delicious indeed, had given Emmagene a light, airy feeling, which often served to loosen her tongue. It had been Geoffrey who had introduced her to whiskey, along with other things. She could still see him standing before her with a bottle he'd pilfered from his father's study. They'd taken turns sipping from it before undressing each other and making love. Her skin rippled at the memory. What would it be like to have Huntly undress her?

"A friend," she answered.

Huntly's eyes pierced her with blue flame in the rapidly fading light. "Ah. A gentleman friend." There was no censure in his tone. No condemnation that Emmagene had been sampling whiskey with a man. And she didn't think Huntly would judge her for her loss of virtue either.

"May I have another sip?"

He nodded, handing her the flask again. "You aren't a sot, are you?"

"What?" Emmagene grabbed the flask, inhaling as he deliberately brushed his fingers against hers. "No. I am not a sot. I happen to enjoy whiskey," she snapped. "Also, cognac and brandy." The smoky caramel of the whiskey bathed her tongue. "I don't care for ratafia or sherry."

"Of course not. Who does?" Huntly, fingers thick and blunt, plucked at the blanket. "When did you learn to enjoy…a good whiskey?"

"I was barely eighteen." The conversation was no longer solely about the appreciation of a fine whiskey. Emmagene stared back at him, daring Huntly to make some innuendo or derisive comment, but he didn't, only continued to gaze at her with a thoughtful look on his rough features. "I haven't enjoyed a good whiskey since."

Huntly's entire body uncurled in her direction, like some giant bear waking up from hibernation, ready to pounce on the unsuspecting rabbit that had the misfortune to hop by him. She understood, with startling clarity, as he studied her with heavy-lidded eyes, how Huntly, though reviled for his ill manners and rudeness, still managed to entice a startling number of women. There was a sensualness to him, well buried but present nonetheless.

A servant arrived bearing a platter of food, interrupting the charged silence between them. Cheese. Fruit. Bits of poached meat. A more substantial meal would be served once the fireworks ended and the guests returned to the house.

Huntly's interest left Emmagene for the platter of food. He regarded the array of tiny plates and their contents with distaste.

"Is there a problem, my lord?" she said, somewhat relieved to have Huntly focused on something other than her. The air around them had grown combustible as if the blanket could catch on fire at any moment. "Surely you are able to throw a slice of apple as well as peas at an unsuspecting servant should it be required. You might need to try lobbing the fruit from a different angle—"

"There isn't anything," he interrupted, one of his large fingers flicking at the tray in dismissal, "robust."

"Robust?" Emmagene plucked a bit of cheese from the tray.

"Yes, Miss Stitch." His deep-blue gaze settled on her lips. "I'm a man of formidable appetites. You should know that."

"I stand forewarned." Emmagene swallowed the cheese, her pulse wavering in her throat. Such wickedness abounded in Huntly's words, particularly when he was eyeing her with such intent, which he made no effort to hide. The animosity between them had shifted subtly into something else entirely. Encouraging it, and him, could be a mistake.

Her gaze trailed over his large, bulky form. The broad shoulders stretching his coat. The thick thighs and chest, heavy with muscle. What would it feel like to have his weight on her? Have him press inside her?

A tiny shiver shot down between her legs.

"Do you want more whiskey, Miss Stitch?"

The low timbre of his voice was better than the taste of chocolate hitting her tongue. Huntly was no stranger to seducing a woman; that much was evident.

"Are you trying to get me foxed, my lord?"

"I doubt very much you can be forced to do anything you don't wish to." He leaned closer to her. "Your eyes aren't watering. The vinegar must be finally wearing off."

It wasn't; it was only that Emmagene's other senses were so overwhelmed she could no longer smell it.

Another servant appeared at Huntly's shoulder. "Wine, my lord?"

Huntly looked over at Emmagene. "Just leave the bottle. I'll serve the lady."

The servant, a young lad who looked frightened by Huntly,

handed him the bottle without another word and disappeared into the maze of other blankets. Torches had been placed at intervals around the area where the other guests were seated, but the light didn't quite reach Emmagene and Huntly.

Emmagene lifted her glass as Huntly poured out the wine, glad to have something to do with her hands. She looked down into the glass, barely able to make out the contents.

"I have a confession to make." He swirled his own wine before taking a swallow, eyes never leaving hers. "Too fruity."

Her skin prickled at his regard. "Is that your confession? The taste of the wine?"

"I meant to kiss you. Wanted to. I won't apologize for it."

Well, that was quite blunt. "You won't?" Fireworks began to light the sky behind her.

"You enjoyed it. Don't be afraid to admit it, Emmie."

Emmagene sucked in a lungful of air at the intimate use of her nickname. Suddenly this entire flirtation with Huntly struck her as ill advised. She stood abruptly, the wine glass tipping in her hand. A crazy sort of panic filled her. She was aroused, frightened, the whiskey casting its bloody glow over her body. And Huntly. "I—"

"Leaving?" he drawled flatly. "I thought you possessed so much *more* backbone, Miss Stitch."

She possessed an *enormous* amount of backbone. Her mother often claimed Emmagene's spine to be forged of steel. Part of her registered the tone of Huntly's voice. Angry, she thought, at her perceived rejection. Emmagene didn't care for it in the least. Because—

A boom sounded, so loud the earth vibrated beneath her feet as a spray of green and gold lit the sky. Startled, she dropped the wine glass and reached to catch it only to trip over the bloody tray of food. A piece of cheese, which honestly hadn't been a very good cheddar, had become wedged under the heel of her slipper. She slipped, falling backward toward the dark, wooded slope of the hill.

"Damn it." Huntly didn't even sit up, only leaned over and reached for her ankle.

A *gentleman* would have stood and come to her aid. She fell over his stretched legs and started to tumble down the incline, Huntly rolling with her and refusing to let go of her ankle.

Emmagene kicked out at his hand. "Let go of me." Her skirt was riding up her thighs in a most embarrassing manner.

Huntly grunted but didn't release her, tumbling down the embankment with her. Bits of dirt, sticks, and leaves caught at her hair and skirts as she and Huntly fell. She heard the rip as one of her petticoats caught on something. His grip tightened as they came to the bottom, Huntly lifting her so that when they finally rolled to a stop, it was he who fell against a boulder, its shadowy outline barely visible, bordering the stream, and not Emmagene.

He let out a grunt as he hit the stone, pulling her to him so Emmagene would be cushioned by his body and not sprawl on the ground. Huntly's breath was heavy, mingling with her own. The fireworks went on bursting brilliantly above their heads. It could take hours before anyone realized they'd gone missing.

Emmagene curled her fingers around the lapels of his coat and pressed her forehead to the warmth of his chest, feeling his arms tighten around her. Her heart beat wildly as much from the sudden fall down the hill as Huntly, who was holding her as if he was afraid she might break.

"Are you hurt, Emmie?"

In answer, she lifted her chin and found his mouth in the dark.

CHAPTER EIGHT

*S*WEET *JESUS.*

Of all the things Henry had thought might happen after sipping whiskey with Miss Stitch, tumbling down a hillside filled with bramble while fireworks were going off hadn't been one of them. When she'd fallen, slipping on a piece of tasteless cheddar, Henry had acted instinctively and grabbed her ankle.

True to form, Miss Stitch had kicked him.

He'd briefly considered letting her travel down the incline without him, before following her down the hill.

Henry pulled her into the circle of his arms as they rolled, knowing of the rocky outcroppings at the edge of the ravine and wanting to protect her. Her forehead had been pressed against his chest, her spare curves molded to his much larger body. Her hair had come loose, the silken strands spraying over his chin and shoulders. When he'd hit the rocks, his nose had fallen against the top of her head, filling his nostrils with honeysuckle.

Now the lush line of her mouth was brushing his, carefully as if he would refuse her. She pulled gently on the edges of his coat, holding him to her.

Henry groaned, pressing her mouth more fully to his own, tasting the whiskey they'd shared on her lips. She was half sprawled on top of him, and now her hips writhed seductively against his, an age-old call for Henry to do more than kiss her.

He pushed her more closely against the rapidly hardening

length of his cock, undeterred by the fall down the hill or the boulder digging into his back. He moved his mouth to the corner of her lips, savoring the sound she made as he found the sensitive skin of her neck. Hand roaming up her spine, he wrapped his fingers around the base of her neck, holding her in place while he nipped along the line of her chin and jaw.

"Emmie," he whispered against the hollow of her neck, rocking his hips forward to press her more tightly against the hardness in his trousers. He turned her slightly, enough so that he could skim one hand up the length of her leg, to her thigh.

The slender body in his arm trembled. She cupped his cheeks and kissed him. Hard. Passionately. Permission for Henry to do what he would.

Trailing his hand over the silk-clad legs, Henry paused with his fingers at the apex of her thighs, the heat of her warming his fingertips. The soft hair covering her mound brushed against his hand as he found the opening in the layers of cotton that encased her.

Henry dipped his forefinger into her damp flesh, circling and teasing until a low moan sounded in the back of her throat. Emmie's inner muscles grabbed at his finger as he thrust gently inside her, her hips grinding against his hand.

God, she's perfect.

He wanted to taste her. Lay her out in the grass while the stream bubbled gently beside them and take her. He wanted her cries of pleasure to echo around him. Hear her laughing. Call out his name as she climaxed. Everything else, including the guests at the top of the hill, faded away until nothing remained but Henry and Emmagene Stitch.

"More," she whispered to him, her legs sliding open further to his questing fingers.

"There they are!" someone shouted.

God. Damn. It.

Henry growled in frustration, pulling his hands from beneath her skirts. He grabbed her roughly, lips claiming hers in a furious kiss. "This isn't over, Miss Stitch." He couldn't see her in the darkness and wished he could.

She slipped away from him, and Henry immediately felt the loss of her warmth atop him.

Lanterns bobbed their way down the hill, headed in their direction.

The crunch of her slippers along with the rustle of her skirts sounded as she stood. "This should never have happened," she muttered. "I was plied with whiskey. I fell. Nothing more. I can't—"

"Why not?" He reached for her in the darkness and found her fingers. "Why shouldn't it?" Grabbing hold of her hand, he pressed an openmouthed kiss to her wrist. "I want you. In my bed, screaming my name as I fuck you. Repeatedly."

"What a romantic you are, my lord." She pulled free of his grasp.

He reached out to her again, and she sidestepped into the darkness. "I will never be anything but honest with you. Would you rather I ply you with compliments? Whisper platitudes in your ear?"

"God, no," she hissed back at him.

Henry stepped back, hearing the bitterness in her response. So that was what had happened to Emmie, this difficult, challenging woman he was beginning to feel so much for and far too quickly.

"Hunt." Montieth, sticks snapping beneath his boots, arrived, the lantern in his hand swinging back and forth, bathing the area in a hazy golden glow. He loomed over them as a tall shadow against the outline of the bushes, stumbling boots and additional lanterns discernable at his back.

"Here," Henry answered Montieth, then lowered his voice. "Emmie—"

"Don't call me that," she whispered back.

"Miss Stitch." Montieth's voice came closer. "Are you injured?"

"Not at all, my lord. A few scrapes. Nothing that can't be mended. The fireworks startled me, and I tripped. Lord Huntly acted very quickly to catch me but didn't succeed."

"I grabbed your ankle," he said to her under his breath. "You tried to kick me off. I suppose I shouldn't have bothered."

Emmie didn't answer. She was already moving off, arm firmly clasped by one of Southwell's footmen.

"I'm fine, by the way, Montieth. Thank you for asking. Took you a while to get here." In truth, Henry wished it had taken hours. "I grew concerned I would need to struggle up the hill in darkness, dragging Miss Stitch."

"Luckily one of the servants returned to ask if you needed more wine. He noticed you were gone, your platter of cheese was smeared all over the blanket, and the wine was spilled. The poor lad debated whether to say anything because he assumed he'd stumbled upon an assignation. I caught him as he made his way to Southwell." Montieth made a chuffing sound that Henry took to be laughter. "I assured him there must have been an accident considering it was Miss Stitch who had been sitting with you. It was far more likely she'd attempted to bludgeon you while watching the fireworks."

"What other explanation could there be?" Henry agreed, trying to make out her thin form as she went back up the hill.

He could still feel Emmie in his arms and taste her on his lips.

CHAPTER NINE

EMMAGENE, ENCASED IN a thick robe after a hot bath, paced back and forth across the rug in her guest room. After arriving at the top of the hill, escorted by one of Southwell's footmen, a brawny young man who'd said not a word to her, Emmagene had been greeted by Lady Trent, who Emmagene was sure had been struggling to contain her hilarity at the notion of Emmagene tumbling into the underbrush with Huntly. The muted horror of the other ladies in attendance had been evident by a scattering of gasps and the snapping of Lady Bainbridge's fan. Honora, bless her, had insisted on personally escorting Emmagene back to Longwood. Of Huntly, there was no sign. He could have been skipping through the woods with Montieth for all she knew.

A hot bath had soothed the aches from her body, and Honora had brought ointment for her scratches, along with a small decanter of brandy. There was nothing to be done for the way her emotions ebbed and flowed, nor the soft press against her heart at the memory of being protected by Huntly's muscular form.

After assuring Honora she was fine, she pushed her cousin out the door.

The lower half of her body gave a delicate throb, a reminder of what would have occurred had Montieth not found them. Sitting beside Huntly on the blanket, sharing whiskey with him, had imbued Emmagene with a warm, tentative glow. A feeling of companionship. Of being known by someone. Silly, she supposed, because they'd known each other less than a week. Her eyelids fluttered closed as she recalled the gentle touch between her thighs. The way he'd cradled her to keep her from harm.

Emmagene hadn't wanted it to end.

Huntly, blunt to a fault, had whispered he wanted to fuck her, words she found both crude and oddly arousing. There would be no false declarations of love in order to bed her. No lies regarding affection, or promises for the future. He wanted Emmagene in his bed and nothing else.

She stopped pacing and looked at herself in the mirror.

Her hair, now free of twigs, flowed over her shoulders. What little curves she had were hidden deep within the folds of her robe. She tilted her head, taking in the pale oval of her face. Under the best circumstances, Emmagene might be considered striking. She would never be thought of as beautiful, like Honora. Nor was her figure anything to become overly excited about. Geoffrey had often mocked her boyish form, though it had not stopped him from taking his pleasure. Yes, she'd allowed a few other gentlemen to steal a kiss here and there but mainly out of curiosity on her part. None of them had truly been interested in Emmagene, only what marriage to her would bring them.

No man in recent memory had wanted Emmagene solely because they'd found her desirable. Except for Huntly.

She was rapidly approaching thirty. Firmly on the shelf. Her status as an older, unwed spinster meant no one cared the least about her reputation. Her virtue might have been in danger had she not already been relieved of her maidenhead by a wastrel son of Lord Anderly. There was absolutely no reason Emmagene shouldn't allow herself a small indiscretion. Wasn't that what house parties were for?

Huntly was unlikely to pursue her once they returned to London, nor would she wish him to. It was doubtful she and Huntly would ever see each other again. Huntly wasn't popular in society, had few friends, and was unlikely to gossip. Besides, who would care about the love life of the sour Emmagene Stitch?

A knock sounded on her door, and she paused in her pacing before the fire. Probably Honora returning to check on her once more. Shaking her head, she flung open the door. "Honora, I promise I am well. It was just a fall. Nothing—Oh."

"Your boundless vocabulary seems to fail you when not cursing."

The Earl of Huntly, massive form filling her doorway, looked down on her, an amused smile fixed on his lips. His gaze ran along the hair streaming over her shoulders, then down her body, to her toes. It felt as if he peeked beneath the hem of her robe. Heat darkened the blue of his eyes a moment before his mouth swooped down to capture hers.

HENRY CONVINCED HIMSELF he would only check on Miss Stitch after their tumble down the hill. They were both in the same, partially deserted wing of Longwood, where Lady Trent put away the most troublesome guests. No one would remark on his presence at her door. He assured himself as he left his room to go to hers that seeing to her welfare was the proper, gentlemanly thing to do.

Not a bit of it was true.

Once she opened the door, clad only in a robe, which frankly did nothing more than entice him to behave poorly, Henry's mouth fell on hers. Ravenous and urgent. He wanted to swallow her whole.

Emmie clung to him, as he'd hoped she would, rising on tiptoe to wrap her arms around his neck. There wasn't anyone to see, at least not where their rooms were located.

He kissed her as if he would never do so again, seeking out the soft recesses of her mouth with his own. His hands wandered down her lithe body, now after much consideration, more perfect for him than he could have imagined. Her sleekness fit against his rough form as if they'd come from the same mold, her small curves malleable beneath his hands. Desire for her threatened to overwhelm him. When he lifted her, she wrapped her legs around his waist without hesitation.

Henry kicked the door shut.

He ran his tongue along the seam of her lips, coaxing her to open her mouth and groaning when she did, breaths and tongues mingling. His cock twitched, the arousal for her threading around Henry's hips and thighs with painful urgency.

Emmie moaned, pressing herself more fully against him.

Henry laid her on the bed and stood back, lust filling him at the sight of the partially opened robe exposing her skin. Her gorgeous hair spread out in a halo around her.

"I won't be gentle," he said in a choked voice, wanting her so badly he could barely speak. "I don't think I can be."

"Good. I can't be either." She tilted her chin at him.

Henry dragged his hands slowly up the lengths of her legs, long and toned as he'd imagined them to be. Moving his hand across her hip, he tugged at the sash of the robe.

She was naked.

Gently Henry trailed a finger over the small, beautifully shaped breasts, lightly grazing a peaked nipple before brushing over the skin of her stomach. His hand splayed just below her navel as he stared down at her, his heart constricting in ways he had never considered. He leaned over, lips trailing along the side of her breast, before placing a kiss on one taut nipple.

A low gasp of pleasure came from her. "I'm no longer a maid."

"I don't care." Henry pushed her legs apart, adoring every perfect part of her. He tore at his trousers, released his aching cock, and thrust into her waiting wetness. His fingers sunk into the silk of her hair, honeysuckle filling his nostrils as he took her, inch by inch. Roughly. Savagely.

Emmie cried out as he filled her, head thrown back against the coverlet. Her hips met every thrust, taking all of him, until Henry was buried deep inside her. Her inner muscles fluttered against his length, struggling to adjust to him, and he nearly slowed, but the feel of her nails on his back urged him toward a more punishing rhythm. Her teeth sunk into his shoulder.

Jesus. Emmagene Stitch might just kill him.

His fingers moved between their bodies, teasing at the sensitive flesh until Emmie panted, begging for her release. Only when she cried out, arching against him, did he allow his own pleasure to overtake him. A near-violent climax of such intensity Henry felt the power of it to the tips of his toes.

"Emmie."

CHAPTER TEN

EMMAGENE OPENED HER eyes to the canopy above the bed, heart still pounding, body throbbing as the last of her climax ebbed from her limbs. The force of their joining had pushed her across the bed. He lay atop her, his large body firmly wedged between her hips.

"Emmie," he whispered, his breath fanning her cheek. "Are you well?"

She blinked at him.

"Oh, good. I was afraid you'd fainted." He brushed her lips with his, carefully leaving her and relieving Emmagene of his weight. "Did I hurt you?"

"No." Quite the contrary. Emmagene felt absolutely marvelous. She'd never been taken with quite so much ferocity before and regretted not one moment.

The bed creaked as he stood.

Emmagene shut her eyes. He would leave now, she supposed. The sound of clothing rustling filled the room. She waited for him to bid her good night, but the door never clicked. Instead, she heard his heavy tread moving about the room. Her eyelids fluttered open.

Huntly was now completely naked, having removed the remainder of his clothing. He'd padded over to the far side of the room, where a fresh basin of water and towels sat. Firelight bathed the lines of his body, glancing over the curve of his buttocks and the heavily muscled thighs.

He turned and winked at her, a towel in his hand.

The heavy, broad torso was covered with dark-blonde hair along with lines of rippling sinew. Huntly's stomach wasn't completely flat but sported the tiniest of paunches, keeping him from masculine perfection. His cock jutted from a nest of hair between his thighs, still half-aroused.

Emmagene stared at Huntly and all his magnificent maleness, wondering how she'd survived being intimate with him. A tiny thrill ran through her at the thought of doing so again.

There was a predatory gleam in his eyes as he returned to the bed, looming over her, massive hand splaying possessively over her stomach before he pressed an openmouthed kiss on the curve of her hip. Taking the damp towel, he washed Emmagene, despite her protests, all the while grazing her hips and thighs with his teeth. When he finished, he tossed aside the towel and trailed his lips along the inside of her thigh, nipping gently at her skin. The tip of his nose nuzzled against her mound, the gesture intimate and incredibly erotic.

Emmagene's pulse skipped in an unsteady rhythm. "Huntly—"

He tossed her leg over one massive shoulder. "Henry." His tongue trailed through her folds. "I think it would be appropriate for you to use my first name, Emmie. Under the circumstances."

She looked down at his shaggy tarnished-gold head of hair nestled between her thighs.

"Henry," she stuttered as he lowered his mouth once more, tongue teasing at the small bit of flesh that throbbed and ached for his touch. A low purr left her, the sound of slowly unwinding pleasure.

"So responsive," he murmured against her thigh. "So beautiful."

His thumb teased along her slit, all the way to the back, pressing and testing.

She jerked at the slight, foreign touch.

He chuckled softly against her, turning his hand to cup her

buttock, the sensation retreating. "The things I will do to you, Miss Stitch."

Frankly, Emmagene couldn't wait. The things he was doing to her now were so painfully blissful she thought she might actually faint this time. She threaded her fingers through his thick curls and stretched her hands across his skull, pulling at his hair.

"Right here?" he whispered, allowing his words to vibrate against the sensitive, swollen nub.

A whimper was her answer.

He toyed endlessly with her, drawing Emmagene to the edge of her release and then pulling back, until she clawed at his shoulders. When he sucked her completely into his mouth, teeth ever so gently grazing her swollen flesh, Emmagene broke into pieces. She turned her head, screaming out her release into the pillow. The tremors still rippled across her skin when he notched himself again between her thighs.

Another wave of pleasure rolled through her as he took her hard again, whispering her name along with a host of filthy, unimaginable pleasures, all of which he meant to share with her.

CHAPTER ELEVEN

N O WONDER THERE were women who pursued the crude and boorish Earl of Huntly with such determination. If Huntly made any effort at all to be charming, women would be wrestling one another to get to him.

She ran her fingers tentatively over his arm, tracing the bands of corded muscle, moving along the line of his broad chest, twisting the crisp dark-blonde hair. He really was rather spectacular. And heavy. A tiny squeak left her as she tried to shift beneath him.

Hearing the sound, Huntly immediately moved to the side, blue eyes full of concern. For her.

"You didn't hurt me," she assured him. "You are only heavy." She cupped his cheek. "I didn't harm you, did I?"

A chuckle, deep and melodious, came from his chest. "No, Miss Stitch, you did not." His hand fell to her hip, stroking circles around her skin.

Emmagene sighed with pleasure at the rough feel of his fingers. Calloused. Probably because Huntly refused to wear gloves. Or remain polite. Pleasant. Gentlemanly. Had Huntly always been this way, or had becoming an earl had something to do with it?

"When did you inherit the title, my lord?"

The fingers halted their perusal. "Shortly after South left to travel the Amazon. My brother's death was sudden. Fell from his favorite horse."

There was a painful lilt to his words, barely noticeable beneath his usual curt way of speaking. But Emmagene heard it all the same.

"A horse I'd gifted him with." An ugly, self-deprecating sound left him. "My parents didn't long survive Douglas." His harshly cut features grew shuttered. "The shock I would become the next earl was too much for both of them."

Huntly abruptly rolled over onto his back, taking Emmagene with him, pushing her legs apart until she straddled him. After pushing himself into a seated position, he leaned over and sucked one of her nipples into his mouth while shoving her very firmly against his rapidly hardening cock.

Emmagene grabbed at his shoulders, whimpering as he licked and nibbled his way over her breast.

"I told you, Miss Stitch, I have a formidable appetite." He lifted her easily before sliding deep inside her again. One hand took hold of her hip as the other floated to the space where their bodies joined. He moved his thumb against her, watching her face.

Emmagene bit her lip. She was going to die from pleasure. Which was a splendid way for him to distract her from any more questions about his family.

"You should put your hands on my shoulders." He thrust firmly up inside her. "And pray we don't break this bed."

CHAPTER TWELVE

EMMAGENE LOOKED DOWN at her hands, the small bouquet of flowers she clutched crushed by the press of her fingers. She barely heard the minister over the steady, frantic beat of her heart. Images flashed in her mind. Her naked body entwined with Huntly's. His mouth on every part of her. The number of times she'd screamed into her pillow from sheer pleasure.

She shifted in the pew, wincing at the slight soreness between her thighs.

Huntly had taken her four times last night before finally leaving her drained and exhausted just before dawn. Her eyes hadn't even opened as he'd let himself out, Emmagene barely registering the possessive cupping of her breast as he'd pressed a kiss on her temple.

"Luscious thing," Huntly had whispered against her ear.

No one, not even Geoffrey in the throes of desire, had *ever* called her luscious.

Emmagene, whether she liked it or not—whether she wished it or not—felt tethered to Huntly now. Part of it, she guessed, was the sheer intensity of being bedded by him.

Her cheeks warmed as if she was standing before a fire.

The other part was the terrible, awful opening of her heart in his direction.

There was no future for her and Huntly. There couldn't possibly be. The very idea of the sharp-tongued spinster and the rumpled, ill-mannered earl was ridiculous. They couldn't even *converse* without arguing. Their attraction was a result of Lady Trent throwing together two undesirable guests at a house party so they wouldn't offend the others in attendance and spoil her event.

Emmagene pictured her suite of rooms in her parents' home. The rows of books lining the walls, all in alphabetical order. The comfortable chair placed at exactly the right angle for the best light from the window. There was charitable work she was fond of, the saving of orphans and such. She had her nieces and nephews, whom she adored. While her parents despaired of her unmarried state, witnessing the lack of suitors and starched behavior of their daughter with mounting chagrin, Mr. and Mrs. Stitch had, for the most part, accepted Emmagene's declaration she would never marry.

Now along came Huntly, the most unlikely of complications, threatening to upend the placid existence she'd planned for herself. She couldn't possibly feel anything romantic for Huntly. Didn't want to. The very thought filled her with the most unreasonable panic.

An image of his head between her thighs flashed before her.

Emmagene swallowed and pressed her knees together again, desperately trying to staunch the sudden ache such thoughts brought. She was at the wedding of her dearest friend and cousin, for goodness' sake. Seated in a pew at a church. Clutching flowers. A vicar was speaking, though not very well.

Huntly had not been at the light luncheon served before the guests had walked the short distance to the church standing at the edge of Southwell's estate. Emmagene had lagged behind the others, hoping to see him, nodding politely to Lady Bainbridge and her dimwitted niece, Miss Cradditch. He wasn't at the church, Emmagene had noticed as she'd taken a seat, alone, near the back. Nor had he arrived with Montieth. It was time she faced the obvious: Huntly, having bedded her last night, would now take great pains to avoid her. Which was what she wanted. Or didn't. She couldn't be sure.

Emmagene tore the head of a daisy clean off the stem.

The vicar droned on, seemingly oblivious to the overly warm air of the church and the guests carefully dabbing their upper lips. She had never in her life heard such a grating, annoying voice. From a vicar, one expected better diction. A more pleasing tone.

Another daisy met the same fate as the first.

The pew creaked with the weight of someone taking a seat next to her. Warmth slid against her side along with the scent of shaving soap with not a hint of vinegar.

"Dear God, what did the bloody daisy ever do to you, Miss Stitch?"

Her pulse skipped, though she willed it not to.

"You're late," she hissed, suddenly overjoyed Huntly was here, next to her. She clutched the daisies tighter.

"I had a rather exhausting evening."

His eyes were very blue in the early afternoon light of the church. And guarded as if he was unsure of his welcome.

"I could barely crawl out of bed this morning and make myself presentable," he growled. "May need a nap after the ceremony. Was hoping you'd join me." He raised a brow. "Stop scowling. We are at a wedding."

"I'm not scowling; I'm composed." A sort of giddiness filled her at his teasing. "And I have a bouquet," she retorted.

"Which you're destroying." He moved his thigh closer so it pressed against hers. They were seated far in the back with no one behind them to see his improper behavior. "I take it you don't like daisies. Or weddings. I don't care for them overmuch either. Mildly surprised lightning didn't strike the church as I entered." He nodded none too discreetly toward the front of the church. "Where do you think they dug up this vicar? He's terrible with that pronounced lisp of his. If I begin to snore, please wake me."

"You are awful."

"You were thinking the same. Shrewish spinster." There was

a tiny tug at the corner of his mouth. He leaned in until his nose brushed the curve of her ear. "Luscious thing."

The ache between her thighs throbbed in response to his words. Emmagene surmised, somewhat unhappily, if she wasn't careful, she would end up like some trained dog. Huntly would need only to whisper to her and she'd become undone.

"He married Southwell's parents, from what I understand," she replied tartly.

"Yes, well I know how that relationship ended." At her look, he said, "Not well. There is a reason South is an only child. His mother was said to have cried tears of joy at producing the requisite heir and immediately set off for London, leaving South with his nursemaid. Mine at least waited until my brother went off to school."

Douglas. It was clear Huntly's parents had blamed him for the death of his brother because Huntly had gifted him the horse, though she didn't think his relationship with the former Earl and Countess of Huntly had ever been warm.

That bloody unwanted tether to Huntly tugged harder in his direction. She fixed her gaze on the front of the church.

Southwell was repeating his vows to Honora, his features full of love and adoration for her. It was so honest, so genuine, she could barely watch. And because Emmagene had been ruined by a lying, spoiled gentleman, she'd nearly helped destroy Honora's relationship with Southwell. Her own experiences had led her to become bitter. Hurling her scathing opinions around to anyone she deemed beneath her, in an effort to protect herself. She'd become hard. Difficult.

Unlovable.

Moisture gathered behind her eyes, and she blinked to dispel it. Perhaps that was truly why she and Huntly were drawn to each other.

A large, warm hand, calloused because he refused to wear gloves, captured her fingers just as a tearful Honora vowed to love Southwell to the end of his days. Emmagene shivered, just slightly, at the remembered feel of those same fingers caressing her skin.

"Didn't promise to obey him, I noticed." Huntly laced his fingers with hers, holding tight as if she'd dash away from him.

"You'll snap my fingers with such a grip." She tried to tug her hand away, suddenly embarrassed by self-pitying thoughts. "I don't need to be comforted."

"No one said you did." His baritone brushed sensually against her skin just as his mouth had done last night. "Stop wiggling about. It's annoying."

Emmagene glared at him.

Huntly glared right back.

She felt immeasurably better.

Finally, the vicar pronounced Southwell and Honora man and wife, the church erupted in cheers as the pair made their way down the aisle. Southwell walked without his cane, carefully and with much determination, Honora matching his steps and holding tightly to his arm.

Huntly squeezed Emmagene's fingers one last time before letting go so he could clap and whistle. He was smiling, something she suspected he did with even less frequency than herself. The light through the windows bathed his rough features, even managing to make his poorly tied cravat shine. Huntly was an attractive man, not ravishingly handsome like Southwell but good-looking enough to cause Emmagene's heart to beat furiously.

The wedding guests all followed behind the newlyweds as they left the church for the walk back to Longwood. Southwell and Honora were assisted into a carriage festooned with ribbons and flowers. All that was missing was the birds singing in their honor and an appearance from the queen to grace the event. It was grand and beautiful. Awe-inspiring. Like something right out of that stupid romance novel Honora had sent Emmagene to read.

A smile froze on her face as a wave of self-awareness filled her. At what an unpleasant person she'd become.

As the carriage drove off and the guests began to drift back to Longwood, she glanced to her left, expecting Huntly to be nearby. His hand had been on her waist as they'd exited the church, and she suddenly, very much, wanted to talk to him.

His large form, easily found, stood beneath an old oak tree near the church. Montieth and he were engaged in conversation, the first she'd seen them have since the house party had started. Miss Cradditch, lavender skirts floating in the breeze, stood between them.

Normally, Emmagene wouldn't give Miss Cradditch a second thought except that the girl was looking at Huntly with a great deal of interest and not Montieth, whose side the little twit hadn't left since this bloody party had begun.

As Emmagene watched, Miss Cradditch giggled, swatting Huntly in a playful manner. Her fingers hovered in the air before finally taking hold of his arm.

Huntly made no effort to hide his displeasure from Miss Cradditch. There was a grimace on his lips, and he looked at her as if her hand was a wasp who'd settled on his arm. But he also didn't shake her fingers away.

The sight of all that giggling and pressing of fingers made Emmagene's stomach pitch. She wanted to fault the breakfast this morning. The eggs had been overdone. The bacon much too greasy for her taste.

She jerked her head from the sight. What business was it of hers if Miss Cradditch formed an attachment to Huntly? Nothing would come of it. Except Huntly, much like his friend Montieth, required a wife at some point. Titles needed heirs, didn't they? And why did it matter to her?

Damn it.

This was what came of opening oneself up. Feelings of rejection. Loss. Annoyance that Miss Cradditch, though a complete idiot, was beautiful. Suitable.

Things Emmagene was not.

She dropped her bouquet, uncaring when she crushed what was left of the daisies beneath her feet, and began the walk back to Longwood. Alone. Tonight there would be dancing. Musicians had been brought from London. A splendid feast would be laid out, buffet-style. Champagne and toasts to the happy couple.

More than enough entertainment to distract her from Huntly.

CHAPTER THIRTEEN

I SHOULD NEVER *have let go of her hand.*

Henry circled South's exhibit hall that tonight was doubling as a ballroom. Lady Trent had lobbied for South to put his collection in storage until the wedding was over, but he had declined. His guests danced around his gruesome death masks from Africa and the small idols of fertility gods from South America. The musicians were hidden behind hand-painted screens from China.

Where is she?

He'd only stopped to speak to Montieth for a moment after leaving the church. Long enough to know that Miss Cradditch would not become the next Countess of Montieth. The girl was so incredibly annoying, worse than the insects plaguing them during dinner on the terrace. Placing a hand on his arm. Chattering away about how lovely the ceremony was all while glancing between him and Montieth and batting her eyes.

He'd nearly swatted at her.

The only thing Henry despised more than mundane, pointless conversation was flirtation for the purpose of making another jealous, which had been Miss Cradditch's sole goal. Her efforts were completely wasted on Montieth. His friend had no interest in Miss Cradditch despite the high hopes of Lady Bainbridge and Lady Trent. Even if Montieth did find Miss Cradditch appealing enough to wed, he had never shown an ounce of possessiveness over any woman in the entire time Henry had known him. Montieth's disinterest in the girl was so plain Henry wondered how Miss Cradditch couldn't have seen it.

When the girl had finally released Henry from her grasp after realizing Montieth wouldn't give a fig about her even if she went about lifting her skirts for the footmen, Henry had turned to find Emmie. He'd wanted to walk with her back to the house. Maybe take her hand again. But perhaps she'd sensed he was considering dragging her into a patch of primroses and tupping her because she was nowhere to be found.

Slippery little spinster.

His need of Miss Emmagene Stitch, cantankerous, unwed lady, hadn't abated in the least since last night. Something that troubled Henry greatly. It wasn't that he didn't believe in love, per se, but he was cautious of any feelings derived for a woman after spending the night between her thighs.

A bloody spectacular event.

It was only that Emmie was so *unexpected*. He hadn't lied when he'd admitted such to her the previous evening. He'd reached for her when he'd awoken this morning, instantly wishing her slender form were next to his. They could argue over what to have for breakfast. Or make love. Henry was honestly at peace with either.

And now she'd gone and run away from him.

When he and Montieth had returned to the estate with the annoyingly talkative Miss Cradditch, the celebration for South and Honora had already begun.

Henry ignored the lavish buffet set out and instead accepted a glass of champagne. Which he detested, but it seemed the polite thing to do.

He spotted Emmie on the other side of the ballroom, clearly avoiding him for some reason.

Troublesome harpy.

He had no earthly idea what to do with her. Well, that wasn't exactly true. There were a great many things he wished to do to her. All of them wicked and filthy. He'd taken great pleasure in whispering each one to her last night. Henry had the inclination to storm across the room, toss her over his shoulder, and just abscond with her. She'd complain the entire time. Probably insult him. But at least she'd be talking to him, which Henry shamefully admitted was much more important to him than bedding her.

Maybe he shouldn't have taken Emmie's hand at the church, but she'd been so forlorn sitting all alone. Henry had been struck with the urge to comfort her, and honestly, there wasn't anyone else he wished to sit beside. None of the other women smelled of honeysuckle. Or snarled back at him with scathing rebukes.

She was frightened of what was growing between them, something Henry was sure didn't sit well with her. Well, he was unsettled too. They'd just have to muck their way through it.

Laughter echoed through the cavernous room. He thought it might be Lady Bainbridge, who with the array of feathers decorating her hair, reminded Henry unpleasantly of his mother. The late Countess of Huntly had been fond of wearing a turban with an enormous ostrich feather erupting from the top. Whenever she'd chastised Henry, which had been often, the feather would dip in accusation, pointing directly at him.

He turned away from the feathered Lady Bainbridge and stared into his champagne. He considered, not for the first time, what sort of person he'd become. His parents had played a large part in forming his character, though he didn't hold them completely at fault. They had simply never cared for him in the least, ignoring or avoiding him as much as possible. Sometimes Henry wondered if he was merely the product of an unfortunate affair. Maybe the former Countess of Huntly had tupped a groom and he was the result. Or he was the unwanted child of one of his father's mistresses, whom his mother had been forced to raise. Or rather, instruct a nanny to raise.

Henry had been left to run wild, a weed growing in the perfect garden of the Earl of Huntly, stepped on and overshadowed by the magnificence of his brother, Douglas. The earl and countess had hardly cared what Henry did or said. After a time, neither had he. There had never been any threats to cut off his allowance or disown him. Henry's parents had barely remembered his existence. It was only when Douglas had died, having been thrown from the horse Henry had gifted him, that they had thought of him. His parents had declared him unfit for the earldom. Boorish. Rude. Careless with his person and others. Behavior unbefitting a gentleman. They'd both died still despising their youngest son.

And Henry had become the worst earl in London.

He finished the champagne and swiped another glass from a passing servant's tray.

Montieth, after having to defend himself in yet another brawl Henry had instigated, had declared he'd had enough. South had barely been speaking to Henry before he'd left for South America, and their relationship hadn't improved all that much since. Yet here Henry was, given another chance to be a decent human being. Today Montieth and he had spoken as the friends they'd once been. South had invited Henry here.

There were times, like tonight, when he wished he could speak to Douglas just one more time. Ask his brother how Henry could be more like him.

Not completely, of course. Douglas had been a bit of a stick in the mud.

Henry swallowed down the rest of the liquid in his glass. Peering across the room, he took in Miss Stitch. Her gown was the color of oversteeped tea, a dull amber that helped her blend in with the wood paneling in the hall.

Good Lord. Who wore such drab colors to a wedding?

Determined spinsters, his mind answered. One he should probably leave well enough alone. She might not want him disrupting the tedium of what had to be a boring existence.

Oh, it's far too late for that, Emmie. He couldn't stay away from her now even if he wanted to.

He stalked cautiously along the edge of the ballroom, nearly toppling over a podium that held a bit of rock encased in a glass dome. It was covered with writing and appeared to be quite old. Examining the stone for a moment, he wondered why in the world South found it important.

"What do you suppose this is?" He nodded toward the rock. "Looks like bird scratches on stone. Do you think it's a secret message of some sort?"

"I've no idea, my lord. An item Lord Southwell brought back from Egypt." Emmie's brow wrinkled. "I think."

The exposed line of her throat—not fully revealed, mind, because she insisted on wearing gowns with ridiculously high necklines—tempted Henry. He'd pressed an openmouthed kiss to that very same spot the previous evening, tasting the warmth of her skin. The vibrant deep chestnut of her hair had once more been tortured into some elaborate braid and tightly coiled around her head, as if in allowing him to bed her, Emmie had immediately felt the need for restraint.

"I would ask you to dance, but I fear I'm not good at it."

She had lovely eyes. The dark sheen trailed down Henry with her usual disdain, which had been absent when he had held her hand at the church.

"Then I am grateful you won't ask."

"The feathers sprouting from Lady Bainbridge's hair are terrifying." Henry nodded across the room. "Looks like an enraged peacock, doesn't she?" He'd had assignations with scores of women and never once had been ignored or dismissed afterward. If he couldn't still feel Emmie writhing beneath him, he would assume he'd dreamed last night, based purely on her disinterest in him.

A tiny half smile crossed her lips. "Lady Bainbridge's headdress is atrocious, though hardly enough to frighten anyone, my lord."

"I detest your hair in braids." No, she'd enjoyed herself last night. The scratches along his back were proof.

"I don't style my hair in such a way to please you." She cast a sideways glance at him. "You should turn your attention to the state of your own clothing. Did a blind man cut your hair?"

Insults were much better than having her avoid him as she'd been doing since the church. Attraction sparked between them—more brilliant than the fireworks they'd witnessed yesterday. If it invoked a tenth of the arousal in her that it did in Henry, he could well understand her trepidation. It was bloody frightening, especially to people like him and Emmie.

"The tightness"—he lifted one hand and lightly touched her head—"puts you in a foul mood." He said the last bit just to annoy her.

"I'm usually in a foul mood, my lord. I doubt my hair has anything to do with it."

He wanted to ask her why she hadn't waited for him at the church today, but he didn't. It was possible he wouldn't care for the answer.

"I've some whiskey." He patted his pocket, sinking his body into a darkened alcove. "Much better than the champagne Lady Trent is serving."

"I don't care for champagne as a rule."

Of course she didn't. Champagne was a drink Emmie would find much too frivolous with all those bubbles tickling her nose. Henry took out the small flask and stepped further into the shadows. There was a small door set into the wall. Knowing South, it was probably filled with mummies and pottery. He wiggled the flask in the air. "Come, Miss Stitch."

She watched him before turning her neck just slightly to see if anyone was looking in their direction. Smoothing her skirts, she took a hesitant step forward and stopped, looking behind her again.

He could have saved her the trouble. No one was looking. "I'll drink it all if you don't hurry up." Frustrated, he shrugged and took a sip from the flask, the whiskey burning all the way down to his stomach. "Fine. Sip champagne and continue to wander about the ballroom like some tragic wren."

The insult propelled her forward, as he'd known it would. "Tragic wren. Who on earth says something like that when describing a lady? Incredibly unkind and not true in the least. My gown is a lovely shade of amber. Like an acorn."

"If you insist. I liken it more to tepid tea."

Her lips twisted, but she still slipped in next to him, so close her skirts curled around his legs. The alcove was suddenly filled with the scent of honeysuckle, which stretched his poor trousers to their limit.

Troublesome little spinster. How he hungered for her. It struck him that his desire for Emmie was unlikely to go away anytime soon. Or ever.

Henry took another drink from the flask, then bent forward, brushing his mouth against the softness of her lips.

A quiver went through her, no doubt from surprise at his action, but she arched her back in his direction all the same. A silent invitation for him to continue.

"Miss Stitch," he breathed against her mouth. "Do you want a sip of the whiskey?"

"Yes." She moved her lips over his, nearly kissing him back but not quite.

Somewhere along the line, she'd learned how to tease a man. Henry didn't judge her for any choices she'd made in her past, but he was feeling very proprietary about her future.

He carefully tipped the flask for her to drink before claiming her mouth again, his tongue running along the inside of her lips. "You were dribbling a bit. I couldn't allow you to waste a drop."

"I don't dribble," came her breathy reply. She pressed her slender form to his, lithe as a cat, palms sliding up his chest.

As much as Henry enjoyed sparring with Emmie, he liked her like this. Soft and welcoming. Whatever she'd been upset over earlier had been resolved. Or maybe she only wanted the whiskey.

He moved his mouth down her cheek, nuzzling against her skin as he nipped and sucked against the side of her neck. He pulled at the small ruffle around the neckline of her bodice with his teeth. "I want you out of this dress, Emmagene. I'll tear it off you if I must." A low sound came from his chest. "I certainly won't miss this drab garment."

"We shouldn't."

He shifted and slid around her, running his hand up her waist to cup one breast. "We most definitely should. Indiscretions are expected at a house party. Let's not disappoint Lady Trent."

CHAPTER FOURTEEN

T HIS WAS A terrible idea.

Despite Emmagene's resolution to put some distance between them, something she'd decided on after seeing Miss Cradditch drooling over him, all Huntly had had to do was wave a flask of whiskey and vow to tear Emmie's clothes off and she'd found herself being kissed and groped in an alcove of Southwell's ballroom. What of her reputation? Anyone could have seen them. She would have been ruined.

Correction: she was already ruined.

She stalked back and forth before the fire in her room, her toes making tracks in the thick rug beneath her feet. The dress had already been discarded with help from the maid who'd been assigned to her. The same girl who'd taken care of Emmagene last night and probably made her bed this morning. If Southwell's servants were prone to gossip, which all servants were, the news that Miss Stitch had entertained a gentleman last night was already circulating belowstairs. There couldn't be any doubt what had occurred in this room last night. Repeatedly. The maid, a drab girl whose teeth stuck out at odd angles, had looked far too smug for Emmagene's taste.

Emmagene plopped down in a chair before the fire and waited, looking up at the clock every so often. Huntly had inferred they would have an assignation this evening. He wanted to tear off her gown with his teeth. Her heart raced at the mere thought of him doing such a thing.

When the first hour passed, Emmagene began to wonder if she'd misunderstood his intentions. Or possibly Huntly had become distracted by something. Or someone.

Miss Cradditch.

Surely not. The girl was a twit.

This was another reason Emmagene steered clear of gentlemen's company for the last ten years. She remembered this sensation quite clearly from her time with Geoffrey. When he'd promised to meet her in the stables but had never arrived. She'd waited for hours, feeling rejected. Unwanted.

Emmagene stalked to the bed and threw back the covers, glaring at the closed door of her room. She smashed a pillow with her fist. If anyone was going to reject the other, it was Emmagene.

An image of Miss Cradditch, fingers on Huntly's arm, flashed before her.

Without thinking, Emmagene tossed on her robe and slipped out of her room, determined to confront Huntly. She would announce an end to their acquaintance before he could unsettle her further. Marching down the hall, robe flapping around her ankles, hair streaming behind her, she went directly to Huntly's door and knocked sharply. When he didn't answer, she twisted the knob, which turned easily in her hand.

Huntly spun toward the door, surprise lighting his eyes. He was buttoning what looked to be a clean shirt, his large fingers moving with efficient grace. "Emmie."

"You," she sputtered, glancing around the room for any sign of Miss Cradditch. The girl was desperate to marry a title. Anyone could see that. Emmagene wouldn't put it past her to try to ruin herself with Huntly and thus ensure her future role as countess.

He raised a brow. "Yes. Me. I'm not sure who else you were expecting. This is my room, after all."

"I've been waiting, like some pathetic wallflower, for you to come to my room and—" She peeked over the side of one chair.

"I came up a few moments ago. Are you looking for something?"

"Not in the least. Good evening." She started back toward the door.

"A servant spilled champagne on me, Emmie, so I changed my shirt. If it had been whiskey, I might have just worn it, since you seem to like whiskey better than champagne."

Her toes dug into the rug at her feet.

"Will you shut the door?" His lips were twitching. If he burst into laughter, she might throw something.

"You find this amusing?" Emmagene suddenly felt very foolish and very angry. Mostly at herself. Nothing good could come of this.

"Emmie, the door," he said quietly, coming to her.

"This is a horrible idea," she whispered. "I should go back to my room." She'd actually been jealous. Worse, of Miss Cradditch. "I—"

Huntly reached around her and shut the door, flicking the lock. "It's all right." He cupped the side of her face, stroking her cheek with one large hand, and pressed a gentle kiss to her forehead. "Why did you leave the church today before I could walk you back?"

Emmagene shook off his hand, feeling herself soften toward him. "You were speaking to Montieth and Miss Cradditch. I didn't want to disturb you."

A slow look of understanding crossed his rough, handsome features. "Miss Cradditch. The annoying twit. Oh, Emmie." A big hand cupped the back of her head.

"I should go," she said again. "This is a mistake, my lord."

"No, it isn't," he whispered.

It wasn't a bloody mistake. She'd been jealous of Miss

Cradditch because the girl had been holding on to his arm and didn't want to admit to it. That was why she'd stormed in here, hair whipping about her and ready to do battle. He should be grateful she hadn't brought anything sharp with her. Probably meant to make a eunuch out of him.

God. Why did that arouse Henry so much?

She pulled away, looking down at her feet.

"This is not a mistake." He knew that now, in his very soul.

Difficult. Crabby little apple. What must he do to convince her?

Henry put his hands on her shoulders, brushing his fingers against the delicate bones of her back and arms. He bought his palms up to her cheeks and pulled her mouth to his.

A small cry left her as she grabbed for him.

Them. This. Would be hard. Difficult. Painful. Henry knew it and didn't care.

He teased his lips with hers, their tongues twisting together as he lowered his hands once again, gently sliding off the robe, which fell to the floor in a heap. Between nibbling at her lips and caressing her breasts, he managed to get her nightgown unbuttoned and off, leaving her naked in his arms. He stroked her back, soothing sounds he hadn't even known he could make coming from him. He trailed his fingers up and down her spine until the tension left her slender body.

Henry came around and stood behind her, running his big hands over her body to cup her breasts, his fingers circling her nipples. The mirror, large and oval, the very one he'd stood before moments ago, reflected their image back.

"How could you possibly think, Emmie, I would want that pale bit of milk, Miss Cradditch? Look at you. You're beautiful." His voice grew rough with emotion. He meant every word.

Her eyes widened, lashes falling over her cheeks as she watched him caress her breasts and stroke the silky skin of her stomach. He skimmed his hand down to the soft hair of her mound and threaded his fingers through the dark strands.

"I'm not beautiful," she sputtered.

"You are." He moved his fingers lower. "And you're mine." Henry wasn't sure why he'd uttered those words, only that he'd needed to hear them. So had Emmie. It was a declaration of sorts for both of them. One that meant he had no intention of allowing her to go back to London without him.

"Henry." His name came out in a low, seductive moan.

He pulled her toward the bed, picked her up, and laid her across it, facing the mirror. He stripped off his clothes and climbed onto the bed behind her, pressing kisses to the backs of her thighs, her buttocks, the small indentation at the base of her spine before moving up the line of her back.

"I'm not even sure I like you," she whispered.

"You do." He caught her eyes in the mirror as his hands roamed over her body. "I'm the only interesting person at the house party."

CHAPTER FIFTEEN

Emmagene was nothing but a mass of sensation and all of it pleasurable. Huntly's big hands traveled over her skin, stroking. Exploring. She'd been shocked when he'd stood her before the mirror. Watching him coax her nipples into sensitive peaks, touch her stomach, and then stroke her between the legs had been…sinful. Delicious. Erotic. He meant to take her facing the mirror, she surmised from the way he positioned her on the bed. She could feel the hard length of him, heated and thick against her backside.

"Somewhat interesting," she murmured.

Twisting the strands of her hair together, Huntly wound them around his wrist and tilted her chin back. His mouth covered hers, drinking her in, savoring Emmagene as he had the whiskey. The lush sensuality of his kiss sent shivers along her skin as did the slide of his fingers between her thighs.

"I want you so much, Emmie." The rasp lit against her ear. "Had I walked you back to the house today, after the wedding, I would have pulled you into the woods and fucked you senseless among the trees."

Her entire body was throbbing as much from his words as the sight of what he was doing to her. His fingers touched. Caressed. Brushed along her hip and between her thighs. Stroked Emmagene until she was wet and wanting.

Reaching the back of her knee, he pushed her leg forward.

"Look." He pressed a kiss to her neck.

Emmagene moaned, watching their reflection as he entered her with exquisite care. He had fondled her body into such a feverish state the slightest touch from his fingers would send her over the edge. Her eyes met Huntly's possessive gaze in the mirror as he thrust into her body, so small and delicate next to his. Trapped in his embrace. Dominated.

"Henry," she whimpered, feeling the tide of pleasure rise inside her.

Huntly entered her slowly, each time deeper, holding her so tightly she couldn't move, controlling the pleasure mounting inside her. He kept her chin tilted toward the mirror, forcing her to see how their bodies moved together with absolute erotic perfection until she shattered, sobbing his name as her release rippled across her skin.

"Oh, Emmie." His voice was hoarse against her throat as he climaxed. Huntly's arms tightened, their limbs twisting like vines around each other.

Emmagene closed her eyes as the tremors left her, at peace for perhaps the first time in her life. The steady beat of his heart against her chest soothed her. His nose had fallen into the curve of her neck, Huntly inhaling her scent with every breath he took. He made no move to withdraw. He stayed firmly inside her while the fire crackled, and she dozed in his arms. One lone tear escaped to trickle down her cheek, though she willed it not to. She'd never known such beauty.

"I should tell you"—the words came out raw, scratching the inside of her throat—"how I came to enjoy…whiskey. If you're awake."

"I am."

She opened her eyes to find him watching her, his expression unreadable.

"He was the son of an earl, as it happens. I met him in my first season. I thought I was in love." She shrugged, surprised at how distant she felt from that time, though the pain of Geoffrey's betrayal still lingered. It had made her who she was, after all.

"He married elsewhere, didn't he? Lied to you."

Emmagene closed her eyes for a moment. "He did."

"I would never judge you, Emmie, for your choices. Or for my not being the first man in your bed." There was a proprietary look in his gaze. "But I do resent this nameless prick for wounding you and causing you to prance about in dull colors."

"I have never pranced in my life, my lord." She snuggled back against him, taking pleasure in his defense of her even though he'd insulted her wardrobe.

"You're well rid of him." Huntly cupped her breast, idly toying with her nipple.

Though he hadn't asked, Emmagene felt the need for Huntly to know. "There hasn't been any…whiskey drinking since."

"I assumed as much." He pressed a kiss to her temple.

"Smug. You are smug, my lord."

"Not overly so." He chuckled softly against her shoulder, pressing small, featherlight kisses against her skin. "I used to admire a more voluptuous form, but I find I don't any longer."

"How nice of you to say." She struggled to keep the hurt note out of her voice even though she knew it was only his blunt way of speaking. A spare bosom. Little flesh on her bones no matter how much she ate. Sharp features.

"I intended no insult, Emmie." His tongue circled the edge of her ear. "I only meant you are so unexpected and *only* that."

"So you've said." As it happened, Huntly was rather unexpected for her as well.

"If you continue to take offense at everything I say, we'll never be able to have a conversation."

"Stop being offensive."

"I've decided I should work on that. Being offensive. Or at least, being less so. I doubt I could ever change completely."

"And difficult."

The Huntly reflected in the mirror had a serious, intent look on his face as he buried his nose in her hair again, inhaling her and making blissful sounds. "Don't worry," he continued. "I'll always speak my mind with alarming bluntness. But I might decide to know someone better before insulting them." He caught her eyes in the mirror. "I've managed to drive away almost everyone who ever cared for me. Some permanently. While I don't intend to like the vast majority of people, including most of the guests at this stupid house party, I need to get on with them better."

There could only be one reason Huntly meant to make himself more palatable, so to speak. "You mean to marry." The very idea made her ill, the thought of Huntly doing what they had just done with some well-bred young lady.

Emmagene's heart thudded hard in her chest. Painfully.

"Unfortunately, it has recently been brought to my attention that I should marry. Duty and all that. My situation, however, is bound to be far more difficult, particularly for the woman in question. I imagine I won't be easy to live with."

The whiskey they'd drunk earlier swirled unpleasantly in her stomach, reminding her, vividly, of how she'd felt upon reading Geoffrey's wedding announcement in the paper. And when she'd seen him and his new wife walking in the park together.

She was being illogical, of course. Huntly *had* to marry. It was his duty, like it or not. Emmagene, firmly on the shelf, self-proclaimed spinster and more than a bit of a shrew, wasn't the sort of woman a titled gentleman would choose as a wife. Nor, she reminded herself, was love and marriage in the cards for her. Discreet indulgences when the mood struck her, yes. But—

"What do you think, Emmie?"

"I'm not sure my opinion is relevant."

This was a conversation Emmagene did not want to have, especially with part of Huntly still buried and pulsing inside her. Should she be pleased he cared for her thoughts on the subject? Or was Huntly so bloody stupid he couldn't see that perhaps now wasn't the time?

She thought the latter.

"I should go back to my room."

"You've no opinion to offer?" His tone was chilly. "No thoughts on my future married state?"

"None whatsoever." Boorish idiot. She envied his ability not to allow his emotions to play a part in the passion they'd just experienced. It was a trick Emmagene realized far too late she hadn't learned. This was why she'd avoided any sort of flirtation. Remained in the background. Kept her bitterness wrapped tightly around her like body armor.

"Fine." He grabbed her chin and kissed her fiercely.

Emmagene crawled from the bed, ignoring the bored, almost angry look in Huntly's narrowed eyes as he watched her dress. What in the world did he have to be put out about? In his mind, he probably expected to tup Emmagene right up until the wedding day. Perhaps remain her lover until he married another woman. Geoffrey had done much the same. She'd left him in the stables that day, rushed home in time for tea only to hear from her mother's lips of his engagement.

She drew her robe over her shoulders, refusing to look in Huntly's direction. She hated that he'd made her want more and wished with all her heart she'd never come to him tonight. Mostly, she cursed herself for her own stupidity in allowing herself to care for Huntly.

"Emmie." He took a deep breath. "I wish you would stay with me."

"Impossible, my lord." She gave him a brilliant smile. "I'm in desperate need of sleep, and we both know I can't be caught with you. Think of the scandal."

She'd entered into this brief interlude with her eyes wide open. He'd never once professed any affection for her. Never lied or given her expectations. She'd done that to herself. Probably more the fault of this wedding and the insipid displays of affection between Honora and Southwell. Emmagene couldn't possibly care for Huntly. She barely knew him. It certainly wasn't love.

Her hands shook as she belted the robe.

Not yet.

But if she allowed this to go further, it would be. At least for her. Unlike her feelings for Geoffrey, which she now could see paled dramatically in comparison, Huntly made Emmagene want to *cling* to him. As if the world would suddenly become that much more appealing if he were next to her.

Frankly, the feeling terrified her.

"I'll see you at breakfast, Miss Stitch."

Huntly lay before her, large, naked, and incredibly male. A thrill ran through her at the sight, the memory of all that hard muscle and carnal intent curling around her.

She abruptly turned away.

If Emmagene didn't leave now, he *would* lure her back into bed despite her resolve. She had to protect herself. It was that sense of self-preservation that propelled her to the door without a backward glance. She was doing the right thing. The only thing.

Shutting the door on Huntly, Emmagene hurried down the hall toward her own room, already concocting a tart explanation should she run across a maid. Sleepwalking. But she needn't have worried. No one was up and about yet.

A note must be written to Honora. Another to Lady Trent. Her trunks needed to be packed, which she could do herself. Panic leaped up her throat. She had to get as far away from the Earl of Huntly as possible lest more irreparable damage be done to her.

After opening the door to her room, she went right to her trunk sitting in the corner and flung it open. Furiously stuffing in her clothing, she recounted all the reasons she didn't like Huntly and how she could not possibly care for him.

Huntly would be sitting alone at breakfast. Or possibly not. Maybe Miss Cradditch would join him. She would be an appropriate wife for him or any other man.

Dear God, Emmagene sounded like a jealous fishwife.

Yet another excellent reason to avoid Huntly.

She meant to leave Longwood at first light.

Chapter Sixteen

Henry lay on the ground, uncaring that he was ruining yet another coat and had leaves in his hair. Looking back toward Peony's enclosure, he could make out, just barely, the small trail of strawberries and bits of apple he'd carefully placed to lure the tiny skunk to him. The idea to visit Peony had struck Henry as he'd sat alone, the only guest still in the breakfast room.

Emmie had never appeared.

He'd shown only mild surprise when South had informed Henry that Miss Emmagene Stitch had left Longwood at first light. But the knowledge had hardened inside him, making it difficult for him to finish his cup of coffee. Emmie didn't want him. He'd shrugged and eaten another piece of toast. Nothing remarkable about the realization, except he'd thought…well, he'd thought there might be a different outcome.

He'd barely finished his toast, which was dry and tasteless as dust in his mouth, when a rather unwelcome confrontation with the new Countess of Southwell had occurred. Henry had had no idea Honora knew so many colorful curse words or could utter them with such vehemence. He wondered if she'd taught Emmagene. His first inclination had been to lash out at Honora, send back a series of scathing, chilly retorts, toss his toast at her, and walk away. Instead, he'd taken a deep breath and asked, in a calm, moderate tone, why Lady Southwell would think him to be such a rotten human being, besides his behavior for the majority of his life and in particular to Miss Stitch.

The first thing Henry had learned was that his interest in Miss Stitch hadn't been as discreet as he'd assumed. Honora was fully aware he'd been tupping her cousin. She didn't approve necessarily, but Emmie had seemed *lighter* after, so she'd said nothing. As impossible as it seemed, she'd had to assume Henry was the reason. Now he'd driven her away with his careless regard to Emmie's person. Didn't he realize, Honora had demanded, how fragile her cousin was?

Fragile wasn't the word Henry would have used to describe Emmagene Stitch, but he'd taken Honora's point.

He'd bungled things with Emmie. Not the bedding her part— that had been nothing short of spectacular—but the discussion of marriage afterward. Looking back on their conversation, Henry had come to the conclusion he hadn't been clear.

Honora was right. He *was* a bloody idiot.

The grass swayed gently to his left. The tip of a black tail streaked with white appeared, bobbing just above a patch of primrose.

He never should have discussed marriage in such a careless manner, knowing what he did of Emmie's past. He had only wanted to gauge her response to the possibility of a more permanent relationship between them. Had tiptoed around the subject and made a mess of things because he'd been too afraid she'd reject him outright. Stupidly, it had never occurred to him that Emmagene wouldn't think she was the lady in question.

Henry knew what the world thought of him; after all, he'd allowed it to happen. Most considered him rude. Careless in his appearance as well as his behavior. Arrogant. But even Henry wasn't so cruel as to discuss wedding one woman while his cock was buried in another. At first, Henry had been furious. Not only that Emmie had left without so much as a bloody note but because after *everything*, Emmie believed he would treat her so harshly. She was completely oblivious to the way he felt about her. About the way they felt about each other.

A tiny black nose poked through the primroses. Then a pointed face. Another strawberry disappeared into Peony's mouth. Henry didn't dare move a muscle as she approached. The skunk and Miss Stitch had quite a bit in common, as it happened. Neither trusted Henry. Emmie wouldn't care for the comparison.

Peony took another step forward and stopped. Her nose twitched at the bit of apple and strawberry in Henry's outstretched palm. The skunk was even now considering whether it would be best to spray Henry, take the offering of fruit, and scurry back into the woods.

"Come now, Peony." He kept his voice low and soothing. "I've already been dismissed once today. Twice if you count by Lady Southwell."

Henry knew how he felt about Emmagene Stitch, but he didn't see any reason to explain the confusing mix of emotions to Honora. Wasn't any of her bloody business. And she'd been swatting at him like a toddler throwing a tantrum. He'd snarled at South to control his wife.

Emmie *was* fragile, didn't Henry understand? Honora had stated. If the Earl of Huntly wasn't up to the challenge of Emmagene Stitch, it would be best if he never saw her again.

Henry considered doing just that. It would be the easiest course of action.

Peony came closer, nosed his hand, and took the strawberry from it. She looked at Henry, the black pebbles that were her eyes glinting in the sunlight. Her tongue scratched against the palm of his hand as she took her treat, no longer frightened of him.

"You see, I can be patient," Henry whispered to the skunk, who was now sniffing at his coat where another strawberry sat in his pocket. She tugged at the fabric before disappearing beneath it, tiny claws scratching at his chest. Finally, she stopped, having found her prize, but she didn't immediately flee. Peony curled up against him to enjoy her strawberry.

As Emmie had curled up next to him last night.

Henry stared up at the trees, feeling the warmth of Peony

caught in his coat. He'd been alone for a great deal of his life, and it hadn't ever bothered him. He didn't find most people to be interesting enough to bother with, especially the women he encountered who were more than happy to eschew talking for the pleasures he offered them in bed.

He hadn't come to this house party with any intention other than surviving it; certainly he hadn't expected to find a woman who attracted him the way Emmagene Stitch did. Henry knew, in his heart, if he never saw Emmie again, he would be lonely the rest of his life.

Still, he didn't rush off to London to claim her. Instead, he walked out into the woods to visit Peony. Immediately laying siege to Castle Stitch would be a mistake. It would put her on the defensive. She'd swathe herself in some hideous gown and twist her hair into knots. Scowl and pierce him with a withering glance.

He would leave tomorrow, as previously planned, and take a few days to decide what he would do.

Emmie wasn't the only one who was wounded.

CHAPTER SEVENTEEN

EMMAGENE SAT IN her chair beneath the window in her parents' parlor, reading the letter from Honora for the second time. Or it may have been the third. Her cousin and new husband were making their way to Egypt. Emmagene envisioned the couple sailing down the Nile, looking at pyramids while delighting each other with obscure historical tidbits only the two of them cared about. It had taken Emmagene a while, but even she had to admit that Honora and Southwell fit together like a pair of puzzle pieces.

The same way Emmagene, ironically, felt she did with Huntly.

She paused and put the letter down.

Ridiculous. She and Huntly did nothing but argue and lob insults at each other.

A hollow feeling spread out across her midsection, something Emmagene struggled to keep at bay whenever Huntly crossed her mind. Which was far more often than she wished in the month since the house party. Some days she was successful.

But not today.

She had fled back to London from Longwood that day before the sun was even up, determined to leave before the rest of the guests, and especially Huntly, woke. Her note to Honora had been explanatory if not exceptionally detailed. The return to London had been accomplished with little fanfare. Huntly hadn't rushed after the coach or tried to stop her. He hadn't appeared at her doorstep in London. He still hadn't.

She reminded herself there was no reason for him to do so.

The house party had been dull, Emmagene had told her mother, who had wondered at her daughter's early arrival home. No one of interest to even have a conversation with. The gentlemen had all been boring. The ladies, with the exception of Honora, tepid at best.

Mrs. Stitch had only nodded as a servant had unloaded Emmagene's trunks, muttering under her breath about her "difficult" daughter.

Huntly, Emmagene told herself as she picked up the threads of her previous pleasing but somewhat dull existence, had only been a brief interruption. A ripple, as it were, in the placid lake of her life. Maybe in time, she would allow herself another brief dalliance, if the mood struck her. The very idea of being bedded by someone other than Huntly didn't appeal to her now, but she was sure, in time, it would. When her emotions were better under control.

She'd thrown herself into charity work upon her return, most of it dull but necessary. There were always orphans and widows to be saved. Clothing and books to be collected. Donations to be made. Emmagene had even received an invitation to one of Lady Trent's luncheons, benefiting a hospital for the poor. A surprise given the lady's opinion of her.

Emmagene had declined to attend, much to her mother's dismay.

On sunny days, Emmagene accompanied her nephew, Albert, to the park, where she helped him sail toy boats in the pond, followed by a picnic on the grass. Though the paths, especially along the Serpentine, were filled with society taking the air, Emmagene had seen no one from the house party except Montieth. They nodded to each other politely from a distance.

Dutiful, unwed daughter that she was, Emmagene went shopping with her mother. She accompanied Mrs. Stitch when she paid calls on her friends, none of whom Emmagene gave a fig about. To be fair, her mother's friends didn't like Emmagene either. Despite her being on her best behavior, they still cast her pitying looks, all the while whispering about Emmagene's shrewish nature and what a trial she must be for her poor mother.

Huntly's name had been mentioned once on one of these outings and only in passing. He'd been in attendance at a ball and was regarded by the matchmaking mamas as a "most eligible bachelor." Lady Kinderton, the source of the gossip and the biscuits they'd nibbled at, which Emmagene had found somewhat stale, had declared she had no idea where Huntly had gotten his boorish reputation. Lady Kinderton assumed it was his appearance, for he was overly large, which gave the impression of gruffness. It couldn't be anything else, for he had charmed every young lady at the ball.

Emmagene took a sip of her tea, admiring how the light shone through the fine bone china. The only way Huntly would be considered charming, possibly, was if he were foxed. *Gruff* was a term best applied to elderly gentlemen, not boorish earls. Lady Kinderton was quite obviously a nitwit. Emmagene had nearly asked if Miss Cradditch was one of those young ladies who found Huntly so fascinating but had bit her tongue.

An image of Huntly the last time she'd seen him loomed before her. Big and naked, growling at her from the bed. She shut her eyes, willing the memory away.

The front door slammed, echoing down the hall. The sound of boots scuffling against the tile of the foyer filtered into the parlor. Who on earth could that be? Her father was in his study. Her mother was out shopping. No one ever called on Emmagene.

"My lord, you cannot barge in without being announced." The annoyed voice of the Stitch family's butler sounded outside the parlor door. "I'm not even sure Miss Stitch is receiving today."

"She'll see *me*." The rumbling baritone echoed in the hall. "Whether she's receiving or not. Lord Huntly to see Miss Stitch.

Announce me. Now."

Emmagene looked up from the letter, grasping the paper so hard she nearly tore the page in two. Lady Kinderton was incorrect. Huntly's manner still had room for improvement.

A polite knock, and the parlor door opened a crack to reveal Jones, the butler, ruffled but determined to maintain his dignity in the face of the visitor.

Emmagene would try to do the same. She'd been thinking of him only moments ago, and now Huntly had appeared. She suddenly realized how woefully ill prepared she was to receive him.

"Miss, there is a Lord Huntly here to see you."

Hands trembling, Emmagene gently placed the cup back atop the saucer without spilling a drop. She lifted her chin and composed herself, torn between the burst of happiness at seeing him and the wound of their last conversation. Well, if Huntly was here to ask Emmagene to be his mistress or form an understanding until he wed some unsuspecting young lady, he was in for something else entirely. She would have him thrown out. Or rather, Emmagene would insist Jones find someone capable of throwing Huntly out.

"I see," she said much more calmly than she felt. "You may show him in, Jones." After carefully folding Honora's letter, she set it aside and sedately faced the arrogant beast at her door.

Huntly strode in, big and blustering, marvelous in a coat two shades darker than his eyes. The thick muscles of his thighs rippled beneath the leather of his riding breeches as he came forward, the tread of his boots barely muffled by the fine Persian carpet beneath his feet. The burnished gold of his hair was neatly and expertly trimmed, the curls no longer rioting around his ears and forehead. Sunlight glinted off the brush of dark-blonde hair along his jaw. He was still in need of a better shave. Or a more fastidious valet. At least his cravat appeared to be twisted properly.

All in all, a vast improvement.

He was so bloody handsome as he paused halfway into the room, looking down his nose at her. Her heart didn't softly flutter at the sight but flapped wildly about, barely contained by her rib cage.

"Stop twisting your hands like a weeping woman." He glared at poor Jones. "No need for you to hover about." He dismissed the butler with a flip of one large paw.

The butler shot Emmagene a flustered look. He would go find her father the moment he shut the door. This was bound to end badly.

"I'll be fine," she said to Jones. "Could you bring a fresh pot of tea?"

"And scones. Maybe some tiny sandwiches. Something *robust*," Huntly said over his shoulder, instantly reminding her of the night she'd tumbled down the hill at Longwood, in his arms. He leisurely strolled around the small parlor, pausing to peruse her mother's knickknacks and a portrait of a Stitch family ancestor.

"Looks sour." Huntly glanced in her direction. "I can see the resemblance."

Emmagene's lips pursed.

Jones had left the door purposefully ajar in case Emmagene should need to call for assistance. Which she very well might. Huntly had started to circle her like a hungry lion.

"I imagined you in a space such as this," he said, the rough scratch of his voice winding around her legs. "Writing your correspondence. Sipping tea. Devising all sorts of boring things to do with tedious people. Maybe saving an orphan or two." The deep-blue eyes grew heated. "But in my vision, you wore much less clothing." He drew out each word. "Barely anything at all."

"I see." Emmagene didn't care for the predatory look gleaming in his eyes. Or the anger.

"I wonder that you do, Miss Stitch. Montieth held a dinner party the other night, or I should say, Lady Trent did," he said conversationally. "I was invited. I didn't really want to go, you understand, since I despise lengthy dinners almost as much as a house party. The food was excellent, but the other guests were barely tolerable. You'll be pleased to know I threw not one pea at anyone. Would have if you were there, of course." He finally settled across from her on the sofa, stretching one arm along the back. The large hands flexed against the cushions. No gloves, of course, despite the obvious improvements to his appearance.

Emmagene felt herself weaken, just slightly, in his direction. She'd missed this. *Him.* Stiffening her spine, she asked, "There weren't any? Peas, I mean."

"No. Only bits of carrot and potatoes. Nothing worthy of my expert marksmanship. No one wants to be pelted with a sliver of carrot. Doesn't have the same impact."

She caught herself wondering if Miss Cradditch had been in attendance but told herself she didn't wish to know. Why didn't Huntly get to the bloody point so she could have him escorted out? "I'm sure the ladies present at Lady Trent's dinner appreciated your tact. Which brings me to the reason for your visit, my lord. I fear you are wasting your time—"

"Clearly," he snapped.

"I've no wish to enter into a sordid relationship with you, my lord."

"Too late."

Emmagene took a deep breath. Pleasure suffused her skin, and she knew it was due to Huntly's presence. "Must you interrupt my every thought? Does it amuse you?"

"Somewhat." He drummed his fingers, glaring at her.

"Why are you here, Lord Huntly? To ask my opinion again? Perhaps of Miss Cradditch?"

"Are you bloody serious, Emmagene?" Huntly's brows rose.

The use of her full name refocused her. "Go back to your balls and dinners. I've no desire to discuss the benefits of any woman whom you might wish to wed. I find it in poor taste that you did so previously. Under the circumstances."

His nostrils flared. "You're an idiot."

Emmagene bristled, wondering if she should throw her tea at him. "I am not an idiot."

"I've missed you dreadfully, Emmie," he interrupted. "And you *are* behaving like an idiot. Miss Cradditch?" He shook his head.

She sucked in a breath, feeling the pressure of her ribs scraping against her rapidly beating heart. "I don't need to be insulted in my own home, my lord." Standing, she smoothed down her skirts and headed toward the door. "If you won't leave, I will. Good day, my lord."

"I detest you in brown." Huntly reached out, thick fingers wrapping around her wrist. "Don't you want to know why I'm here?"

"I do not."

"Yes, you do. You're bubbling with curiosity. You just don't want to admit it. Rattling on about Miss Cradditch. I've completely forgotten what the girl even looked like."

"Let go." Emmagene tugged at her hand, all the emotions she'd kept restrained threatening to tumble out of her in a painful rush.

"I don't want to let go of you. Ever. Are you blind or just in denial?"

"Neither." Moisture was gathering behind her eyes, threatening to spill down her cheeks.

"I promised that harridan you call a cousin I would be patient. Gentle." His thumb smoothed along the inside of her wrist. "I allowed myself a good amount of time for my anger to cool. When you left Longwood"—his voice thickened—"I found it quite painful."

A tear slipped down her cheek, and she wiped it furiously away.

"Jesus, Emmie." He tugged her, protesting and sputtering, into his lap. His nose glanced along her neck and into her hair. "I'm afraid too," he whispered. "Terrified. Like you. It's why it took me so long to call—well, that and the anger."

She shook her head in denial even as he pulled her against the solid wall of his chest. He smelled of fresh air and a bit of horse. He'd been out riding before coming to her. "I'm not afraid. You are rude and impolite. I'm just—"

"Difficult. Contrary. Opinionated. Wizened like every other elderly spinster in London." His chest rose beneath her cheek as he took a deep breath. "I regret to inform you, Miss Stitch, that I still desire you above anyone else. Even Miss Cradditch." She struggled against him, and he pulled her tighter. "I wish to God I didn't, but I do." His lips grazed her temple. "Don't you find we fit together, Emmie?"

"Stop." She slapped at his chest. Hope. Panic. Fear. They all welled up inside her. "You're only saying this because—"

"I want to fuck you? Of course I do. That should come as no surprise. We especially fit together well when we're naked. But that isn't all I want. You know that in here." He placed a big palm against her heart and took the opportunity to cup her breast.

"No."

"I am"—his voice broke—"so *lonely* without you, Emmagene Stitch. And I can't bear it."

A sob left her, the painful opening of her heart stealing her breath. "Henry, you can't be serious."

"I assure you, I am incredibly serious. I've already spoken to your father, the esteemed Mr. Stitch. Didn't you wonder why he wasn't rushing in here with a brace of footmen to defend you?"

"You've met my father? Why in the world—"

"Interrupted a game of chess he was playing at his club. Told him I meant to court you with the intent to make you my countess. I know you are past the age of consent. Well past. But I want to do things properly. Mr. Stitch was somewhat flabbergasted by my request. Stunned. He kept asking if I meant *his* daughter. I assured him I meant you, Emmagene Stitch."

Her poor father, being confronted by Huntly while merely enjoying himself at his club.

"You must have caused quite a stir," she said quietly into his coat.

"Somewhat. Mr. Stitch sputtered. Coughed on his brandy. But I made myself very clear. So I'll subject myself to strolling in the park. Carriage rides. Ices"—he made a face—"at Gunter's. Looking at you with worship from across a room. I'll even attempt to dance. Whatever it is that makes you happy."

He made her happy. Another tear slid down her cheek. "I don't know if I can do this, Henry."

Huntly pulled her close, one hand stroking up and down her back. "You can. In return for bestowing my affections on you, I expect you to wear something other than various shades of brown, indigo, and gray. A neckline that doesn't stretch up to the bottoms of your ears. Possibly relax the style of your hair. A small trade-off, don't you think, for a blissful future?"

"Blissful." The word choked out of her. "Henry, we will be like a carriage accident in the middle of Bond Street. Unlikely but disastrous. Everyone will stare."

"Let them. We will stare right back." He tucked her beneath his chin, tugging up her legs so they dangled from his lap. "I knew we belonged together from the first moment I kissed you. I won't lie and tell you I was happy about it. Because I wasn't." He paused. "I'm no great prize, Emmie. As I'm certain you're aware."

"Neither am I," she murmured. "Shrewish spinster that I am."

"See? We are a most suitable match. But if it takes a while for you to be convinced before you're ready to hear me say the words that are inside me, before you can trust I won't leave you, then I'll wait, Emmie. For a lifetime if I must."

EPILOGUE

"Y OU'RE VERY MUCH like Peony. I can't believe you don't see the resemblance."

Emmagene peered across the carriage at the Earl of Huntly, trying to keep from laughing out loud. She did that often as of late. Laughed. Giggled. There had even been a few hearty chuckles the other day.

"You realize you are comparing me to a skunk, don't you?" Emmagene brushed the plush velvet of her bottle-green skirts, admiring the black piping along the hem. The heart-shaped neckline clung to the gentle curves of her breasts before squeezing her waist and falling into waves of fabric around her legs. A great deal of her arms and chest were exposed.

"I approve the gown, by the way. Lovely to see a bit of skin, Miss Stitch. You aren't nearly as shriveled as a spinster ought to be."

Emmagene wouldn't be a spinster much longer; in fact, she would be the Countess of Huntly, though she hadn't informed him yet of her decision. Their courtship over the last month had been difficult at first, mainly because Emmagene had refused to believe he was serious. But Huntly, true to his word, hadn't done or said anything that would lead her to doubt him. Most telling was the fact he adamantly refused to touch her beyond a chaste peck on the cheek or the backs of her knuckles. He seemed determined to prove himself to her.

The knowledge he cared so deeply filled Emmagene with the most imaginable bliss.

"I'm glad you like it." She took in his dark evening wear, which made his hair shine a deeper gold. He was big and imposing. Bloody attractive. He was even seated across from her in the backward-facing seat, something he hated but did for her without being asked.

"I ordered nothing in brown or gray, as I promised." Emmagene clasped her fingers in her lap. "There is one gown of deep indigo, but the neckline is indecent."

"Good. Are you wearing the stockings I sent you?" Huntly was eyeing her with no small amount of lust, something he struggled to control but had little success in doing.

Emmagene didn't mind. She flourished and bloomed under his attention, feeling desirable and beautiful for the first time in her life. It was a heady feeling. She was also in love. Deeply. Honestly.

"I am." The stockings in question were made of the finest silk and decorated with small hearts on the ankles and two more at her knees. Very suggestive. She wasn't sure where he'd gotten them. There was little else beneath her petticoat but the scandalous silk against her legs, a little surprise for Huntly.

Emmagene meant to give Huntly his answer tonight and seal his proposal of marriage with more than a kiss. She'd endured sedate strolls. A ball or two in which Huntly had brought his flask, so they'd snuck away and shared a sip, but nothing else. He took her to the theater but not the opera, by mutual agreement. They'd gone riding, but after seeing Emmagene sit on a horse, Huntly had suggested she cancel the riding habit she'd ordered. He'd even taken her to a notorious gambling hell, where he'd taught her how to throw dice.

Her parents' relief at the idea of Emmagene marrying was enough to force them to keep their distance. She was far too old for a chaperone at any rate. Not a word of protest ever crossed her mother's lips when Huntly arrived for Emmagene in his carriage. Tonight she and Huntly were to attend a gathering at Lady Trent's sure to be not the least amusing.

"Show me," he growled.

"Yes, my lord. I will." Emmagene dragged her skirts up her legs with exquisite slowness, the velvet tickling her silk-clad calves. It was an incredibly erotic sensation, which would be made better if his fingers followed.

"How obedient. Very unlike you."

"That isn't exactly what I meant." She inched her skirts up to her knees, spreading her legs just slightly apart.

His gaze trailed over her ankles, to her thighs, as his breathing hitched. "What exactly is it you are referring to if not the stockings?"

"I'll marry you, Henry. Gladly. Willingly."

"About bloody time." He grabbed Emmagene, pulling her across the aisle. Her skirts spilled across his lap as he turned her until she straddled him. Big hands, no gloves in sight, ran up the silk covering her legs. "You're sure?"

"I am." She brushed her lips against his. "Should we move across the aisle? I know you don't care to sit on this side of the carriage."

"I don't mind as much with you on top of me." His features softened as he cupped her face, slanting his mouth tenderly over hers. "Just like Peony, only I didn't have to use strawberries."

Huntly had shared with her the day he'd lured the skunk into trusting him with strawberries and apples. She didn't care for the comparison, no matter how apt it might be. He'd been hurt and angry that day. Wounded, Emmagene had left him at the first opportunity. She vowed to never hurt him like that again.

Inhaling softly, he trailed his mouth along her jaw. "I could die from wanting you, Emmie. I've been so desperate I even considered conversing with Miss Cradditch to compel you to say yes."

Emmagene bit his bottom lip. "You wouldn't last more than a few minutes in her company before slumping over in complete boredom." She took his hand and moved it further beneath her skirts, to the apex of her thighs.

"You've forgotten your underthings, Miss Stitch."

"Observant. One of your best traits," she whispered against his ear.

"Is all this wetness for me?" he rasped against the corner of her mouth before kissing her again with gentle urgency. "Are you sure, my love?"

My love. Emmagene had never thought to hear those words from any man, at least not sincerely. Never would she have guessed it would be Huntly who would make her believe them.

"I've never been surer of anything or anyone in my life, Henry Eldrick, Earl of Huntly." Her throat refused to work for a moment. "I love you, Henry." She kissed his cheek.

Reaching up, he rapped a large knuckle against the roof. "We've changed our mind about attending Lady Trent's gathering this evening. Take us through the park. Slowly."

Emmagene's fingers fell to the front of his trousers, and she worked the buttons until his cock sprang free, warm and thick, into her hand. She eased him inside her, biting her lip to keep from crying out at the feel of him there.

He rocked his hips, holding her tight. "I love you, Emmagene Stitch."

About the Author

Kathleen Ayers is the bestselling author of steamy Regency and Victorian romance. She's been a hopeful romantic and romance reader since buying Sweet Savage Love at a garage sale when she was fourteen while her mother was busy looking at antique animal planters. She has a weakness for tortured, witty alpha males who can't help falling for intelligent, sassy heroines.

A Texas transplant (from Pennsylvania) Kathleen spends most of her summers attempting to grow tomatoes (a wasted effort) and floating in her backyard pool with her two dogs, husband and son. When not writing she likes to visit her "happy place" (Newport, RI.), wine bars, make homemade pizza on the grill, and perfect her charcuterie board skills. Visit her at www.kathleenayers.com.